# "I LIVE AND BREATHE UNDER THE MOON

## AND WHEN YOU CROSS THAT BRIDGE...

# "I'LL COME FIND YOU"

"STAY AWAKE" BY LONDON GRAMMAR

**THE BOOKS of MARVELLA**

*With many thanks! Enjoy!*

# GLORY

### A NOVEL

**TRAVIS THRASHER**

LUCAS LANE

Copyright © 2017 by Travis Thrasher. All rights reserved.

Published by Lucas Lane Publishers

ISBN 978-0-9964747-2-6

Cover design by Studio Gearbox

Interior design by Dean H. Renninger

Unless otherwise indicated, all Scripture quotations are taken from the *Holy Bible*, New Living Translation, copyright © 1996, 2004, 2015 by Tyndale House Foundation. Used by permission of Tyndale House Publishers, Inc., Carol Stream, IL 60188. All rights reserved.

Scripture quotations marked NIV and Luke 1:79 in chapter 61 are taken from the *Holy Bible, New International Version,*® *NIV.*® Copyright © 1973, 1978, 1984, 2011 by Biblica, Inc.® Used by permission. All rights reserved worldwide.

Some of the anecdotal illustrations in this book are true to life and are included with the permission of the persons involved. All other illustrations are composites of real situations, and any resemblance to people living or dead is coincidental.

Printed in the United States of America

23 22 21 20 19 18 17
7 6 5 4 3 2 1

THIS SERIES IS DEDICATED TO MASTERPIECE MINISTRIES

THIS BOOK IS DEDICATED TO THE LIFE AND LEGACY OF KENNY KING, WHO PASSED AWAY ON MAY 25, 2016, AT THE AGE OF TWENTY-FIVE. KENNY'S "LIFE MISSION" WAS "TO COMMUNICATE CLEARLY AND CREATIVELY THE TRUTH ABOUT GOD'S LOVE AND HIS PROVISION TO HAVE A RELATIONSHIP WITH CHRIST." HIS DESIRE IN HIS WRITING AND ALL HIS ARTS WAS SIMPLY TO GIVE GLORY AND HONOR TO GOD. HE'S AN INSPIRATION AND INSPIRES ME WITH MY OWN WRITING.

**MOSES SAID THIS ABOUT THE TRIBE OF ASHER: . . .**

"THERE NO ONE THE ISRAEL.

# IS LIKE GOD OF

**HE RIDES ACROSS THE HEAVENS TO HELP YOU, ACROSS THE SKIES IN MAJESTIC SPLENDOR. THE ETERNAL GOD IS YOUR REFUGE, AND HIS EVERLASTING ARMS ARE UNDER YOU.'"**

DEUTERONOMY 33:24, 26-27

# 1

So let me tell you about Marvel Garcia.

There's just something about her smile, something in the way it latches on to you and doesn't let go. It remains in your heart even after she's gone. Calling it warm is like saying the sun is warm. It's not just that it's bright, but that it puts a spotlight on places inside of yourself that you didn't even know were there.

There's the way she carries herself, like some kind of angel in search of a person to rescue. Strong and confident, not a hint of the frightening backstory that might have broken someone else.

There is her fashion sense, which is all her own. It's not just the seventies thing she has going on, it's the way she wears it. The way she walks. The way she blows in and out like some kind of colorful flag on a battlefield.

A guy like me might have someone like Marvel walk through the door to his life, but he knows she won't stay long.

She won't fall for him. She won't give him her heart. But Marvel sorta did. And the sorta casts a long shadow. The sorta changed me.

When Marvel walked into my life, I desperately and foolishly tried to hold on to her, in any way I could, even though I knew she wasn't mine to have.

Marvel was meant for something else. She belonged to someone else. But that didn't stop me.

People talk about being reckless in love. I guess that applies here. Marvel was never reckless, however. She simply gave love back.

But sometimes there's more to the picture. A lot more. Sometimes you have to learn the hard way.

I stare outside a window at the bleak winter landscape.

The February days are dark and cold and windy, and I swear the same snow has been on the ground for a month. Looking dirty with salt and grime and resolve, like it's not about to go anywhere. This morning a fresh batch arrived, covering up the old, ugly scenery with white and light powder. The grime is gone—at least for the moment.

I think about Devon every day. Numerous times. He's been gone since Halloween, but now I know for sure that he's not coming back. The little candle of hope for his return has not only been blown out, it's been buried six feet underground. The funeral was seven days ago, but in my head the music is still playing and my tears are still running and there's nothing to do but close my eyes and pray to God to help us through this.

At school there's a sadness to almost everything, as if around every corner or behind every closed locker or before every spoken word, grief might spill out. A teacher will suddenly get emotional. A student starts crying. A memory reminds us of the tall kid we took for granted, the guy who might speak his mind and gets just a shrug in return.

Nobody shrugs now. It scares people, what happened to him. The other day a routine drill for a school shooting that we do five times a year brought our emotionless principal to tears.

I'm getting to know a familiar friend called sorrow. He doesn't have to knock at the front door because he can just slip in through a broken window upstairs.

I scan our driveway that needs shoveling and the street that needs plowing. But all I'm really looking for is to make sure they're gone. To make sure I don't see either of them—my dad or Marvel's uncle—walking out of the blizzard and back into my life.

The fact that they're somewhere out there and Devon is not only makes the world feel a little more dark.

Nobody has seen my father since he hit my brother Alex and I struck him back with a lamp over the head. We don't know if he's dead or in Mexico or right down the street.

Marvel's uncle vanished too, after he took me downtown and tried to kill me. Maybe he'll never step foot around our suburb again, though I can't imagine he's just going to move on.

I don't think either of them will. I think my dad wants to come back to hurt me, and Uncle Carlos wants much more than that.

The house is quiet. Mom will be waking up soon, followed by my brothers.

There's a family picture on the living room wall, a snapshot of the five of us. All of us boys are so young in the photo, about ten, seven, and five, I'd guess. Even then it's remarkable how close in height Alex and Carter are. Alex isn't just the middle brother but the smallest, too. My mother and father are smiling, but their smiles looked strained. I've never noticed it before, but I can see it now.

The other thing I've never noticed is how much I resemble my father. I don't even want to think about that.

I hope he never comes back to this house.

I'm afraid of what will happen if he does. Not afraid for me, but for him.

# 3

"It's another snow day," Marvel tells me.

I sigh into my cell phone. "I think I'm the only guy in high school who hates snow days."

"Don't be a hater," she says.

"Can't help it. I hate not seeing you."

"Remember our last snow day? We spent it at the mall."

I smile. It's good to have a few fine memories stored away in your pocket. They're like snacks to eat while you're stranded on some island in the Pacific.

"Are the cops still watching you?" I ask.

"Every now and then I see one. But they're probably too busy to keep watching all the time."

After Uncle Carlos disappeared, Marvel and her aunt were kept under twenty-four-hour surveillance. Carlos is wanted for the murders of Devon, Artie Duncan, and Kim Barawski. Artie was a kid going to my high school who was found drowned and cut up in the Fox River last summer, and Kim is a girl from a nearby suburb who was found not long after that. After I gave the police all the details about Uncle Carlos's attempt to kill me, he's wanted by homicide investigators as a person of interest in the murders of these three students.

Wanted for the murders . . . Person of interest . . . It sounds so televisionish, so *Law & Order: Appleton Style*. But it's serious stuff, and that's why Marvel and her aunt moved out of their apartment and are now staying with a cousin fifteen minutes from my house.

"Any leads? Any signs? Anything you've heard?"

"No," Marvel says. "But I did have a dream last night."

"About what?"

"We were at Lollapalooza together."

"That already happened."

"No. This summer."

"Oh," I say. "I like that dream."

"It was just the two of us. We were listening to London Grammar perform right in front of us. It was nice."

"And then it started to rain down frogs from heaven," I joke. "Right? Or maybe hail? Locusts?"

"No. I think I must've woken up before that happened."

"I miss you," I tell her.

"I miss you too."

"No—listen. I really miss you. Like just knowing the living, breathing voice I'm talking to is you. Knowing that all the thoughts inside my head are ones you've probably already thought."

"Wow," she says in a slow way.

"What?"

"You're full of thoughts today, Brandon Jeffrey."

"I always am."

"I know that."

"I didn't know that this thing inside—this love—could actually hurt."

She laughs. "So you're saying I make you hurt?"

"A little," I reply.

Or a lot, if I'm completely honest.

"I don't want to take away from your life," Marvel says.

"I don't think I was really living one until you arrived."

"Don't put me on a pedestal," she says.

"Why?"

"Because nobody should ever be that high up. It'll hurt even more when it comes crashing down."

"As long as you land in my arms, I'll be fine."

"You sound like some romance novel," Marvel says, and I don't answer. "Remember at the record store when we were first working together?"

"Of course," I say. "When you were getting paid and I wasn't."

"Your choice, remember?"

I laugh. "I'd do it again. In a heartbeat."

"Well, I remember how you'd always mumble under your breath. How you had a hard time looking me in the eye."

"Never," I reply with a big grin.

"How you'd never finish a thought."

"Yeah."

"You don't have that problem anymore."

"My only problem is which thought to share with you next," I say. "I have so many."

"I'm not going anywhere, you know. At least not now."

I smile. My cell phone is like an IV on this cold, gloomy,

wintry day. I want to get lost inside it. And I want Marvel to find me there.

An hour vanishes like a snowflake landing on the tip of a tongue. Before we say our good-byes, the inevitable awful stuff comes up.

"Where do you think your father is?" Marvel asks.

I've already made so many jokes about Uncle Carlos and my dad hanging out together that it no longer feels remotely funny.

"I don't know."

"Do you think he's close by?"

"Yeah," I say. "In a drunken stupor somewhere. I'm sure about that."

There's a pause.

"What?" I ask.

"Nothing."

"When you pause, there's always a something."

"I'm just thinking—what it would have been like if we'd met in the normal world?"

I chuckle. "The normal world. Yeah. I remember that place."

"Everything changed the night my father went crazy. The night God spoke to me. Everything. But that awful, terrible thing brought me to you. So there are good things even in the darkest of circumstances."

"Yeah."

It still amazes me how she can look at the world through such a lens.

"I just wish there wasn't some kind of terror waiting out there," she says. "I wish we could just be left alone."

"I like that," I say.

"What?"

"You said 'we.' I like when you talk about us."

"I like us."

"I love us," I say.

"Yeah, I do too."

"Maybe we'll escape this awful stuff. And maybe God will change his mind."

Marvel doesn't need to ask what about. She knows. She's known ever since she heard from God that one day in the depths of her despair.

God can do whatever he wants. Right? So if he wants—maybe, just maybe, he could change his mind.

"Days like this make me sleepy," she says.

"I wish you could take a nap in my arms."

"I'd like that," she says, in a mellow, faraway voice. "I'd like that a lot."

"One day, Marvel."

I add it to my list of things I long for and would do anything to make happen. It's a long list. But everything on it involves Marvel.

"Well, have a good day," she says.

"Can I call you later?"

She laughs. "Sure. Will there be stuff to talk about?"

"There's always stuff to talk about."

"We can just sit here in silence. That's okay too."

I think about teasing her about using up the minutes on her phone, but I don't. I don't say anything.

I like that idea, just the two of us sitting here in the silence.

Just knowing the other is there. Not too far away.
Present in mind and soul and heart.
It's a cool thought to end our conversation on.

# 4

I open my eyes and realize they've been closed for ten minutes. I fell asleep, laptop open, on the couch in the family room. I shake my head like a big old dog and decide I'm as comfortable here as I'd be in bed.

Before closing my computer, I check Marvel's Facebook page, then go to her blog. Sure enough, there's a new post sitting like a lone present under the Christmas tree. It doesn't have my name on it, but that doesn't mean I can't rip it open to read.

The title is "The White-Splashed Picket Fence." I'm already smiling. I can't help it.

> In the deep waters of silence, I ache
>
> Longing for something that shouldn't arrive
>
> Thinking about a distant tomorrow
>
> Wishing for a picture-perfect place not meant for me

## GLORY

The corner crossed between sidewalks

Green grass surrounded by that picket fence

A building, a structure, a home, a heart

And all of it there

All of it somehow there

Blinking I see it

Breathing I feel it

Lost in petals and songs and candlelight

Dreams of the young finally naked and real

Lost in something good and God-given and glorious

Lost in you

Yet I open my eyes and know

I shiver and I realize

These things are not meant to be

They are not meant for me

They just won't be

That voice silences these dreams

And it's okay

I tell myself it's okay

The spirit often reminds me too

But sometimes

Like now

> I long like no other
>
> Desperate to simply have one lovely day

As always, I want to clutch my beating, racing heart and calm it down a bit.

Marvel's words speak to me late at night even though I can't hear a thing. But I know her words, and these don't sound like her. They sound sad. More than that, they sound aching.

I reread them. Each word. And I wonder what she's doing now. How heavy her heart might feel. What she might be dreaming about.

Then something comes over me. This foolish little dream I've had. I even told her about it once.

But tonight—right now—I decide it's not some silly teen dream.

Some teenagers are out there acting their age. But Marvel's older and wiser and I'm just . . . I'm her companion who loves her.

Age means nothing. Age floated down the stream the day she walked into the store.

Reality did the same.

Because I know now what I knew then but couldn't yet understand. That I'm meant for Marvel and Marvel is meant for me and these things she dreams about but knows will never happen *can* actually happen.

"I'll make them happen."

I say this out loud because things are sometimes better when they burst the silence surrounding you. I say it for myself. For the demons that might surround me. For the whatever-might-happen that seems to overshadow us.

"It can happen, Marvel."

This is what I say. This is what I know.

The petals and the songs and the candlelight can be real. The picket fence can surround us.

We can find that place. We can awaken to that lovely day.

I know now this is all I'll try to do. To protect her and finally allow her to be what she wants to be.

Marvel's wishes can be realized.

# 5

When a fight breaks out during lunch hour, I expect to see Greg Packard in the middle of the pile. But it's not Greg; it's a kid I don't know. A younger kid, maybe a freshman or a sophomore. Then I see Seth Belcher, everybody's favorite whipping boy, rushing out of the cafeteria holding his nose. A teacher has the other kid by the collar.

"Who is that?" Frankie asks without interest.

"I think it's Logan Castle or Cessel or something like that," Barton says. He stuffs another handful of chips into his mouth.

Our group of four has gone to three. Frankie is a close friend, a star quarterback (at least he used to be), and an all-around nice guy. Barton, on the other hand, is the comic relief, the lovable moron straight out of *Saturday Night Live*.

"What grade is he?" I ask.

"Freshman, I think."

"What's he have against Seth?"

Barton shrugs. "Nobody likes that weirdo."

"Hey." I jerk my head toward him.

"What?"

Barton's face is round enough to resemble a doughnut, and you can't hate doughnuts. They're not good for you but they sure are yummy.

"Lay off the guy," I tell him.

"Why are you so defensive?"

"'Cause it just seems like the popular thing to pick on someone like Seth."

"Bet he said something to make Logan punch him in the face."

"You're an idiot."

"What?"

I shake my head. Barton doesn't get it, and even if he did he wouldn't care.

As I get up to go in search of Seth, I have an awful thought: *Why did Devon have to be the one to get killed, and leave me stuck with Barton?*

But I stop myself right there. That's crazy. Anybody who dies is missed. Devon had his moments too. I shouldn't suddenly invent ways to miss him.

"Where are you going?" Frankie asks.

"To see if Seth needs help."

"Help with what?"

I look at Frankie, the quarterback with his throwing arm still healing. He blames Seth, but I wonder if he blames me too. He got involved in this mess because of me.

"I don't know," I say. "Maybe he just needs a friend."

"Awww," Barton says.

"You okay?"

Seth doesn't answer. He barely looks at me. He's holding a wad of wet toilet paper on his face, and the tissue is starting to fall apart in his hand. His white Metallica T-shirt with *And Justice for All* emblazoned on it is soaked with water and spotted with specks of blood.

"You get punched in the nose?" I ask.

"It's not my ear bleeding."

His eyes are wet, and I can't tell if it's from the water or from tears.

"What happened?"

"Some young punk trying to be cool."

"What'd he do?"

"Just mouthed off to make the girls laugh. And when I told him what I thought about him, he went off on me."

"What'd you say?" I ask.

So Seth tells me and yeah, I understand why the kid punched him. Seth's comment was pretty nasty. The kind of nasty that goes beyond mean, the kind that's racist and uses words that even guys like Greg Packard probably don't use.

"That's pretty harsh," I say.

"Yeah, well, that's what I was thinking and I stick by it."

"You can't go around saying things like that. It'll get you suspended."

Seth looks at me with disbelieving eyes. Then he laughs and spits on the floor. "Don't," he says.

"Don't what?"

"Don't be all high and mighty. Don't be like them."

I shake my head. "I'm not being like anyone. I'm just

explaining why you can't say loaded words like that. It'll get you in serious trouble."

"You think I care?"

"You *want* to get kicked out of school?" I ask.

"You think I care?" he says again.

"About what?"

"About anything. About anybody. About any of that."

He throws away the shreds of paper.

"Seth, man—I just keep trying—"

"Well, don't," he yells as he jerks away from me. "Don't keep trying. Okay? I'm fine. I'm really terrific. You don't have to do anything. You got it?"

I don't know what to say. It's pretty irritating, to be honest. He's been saying this ever since I met him, and I've continued to ignore it.

"Look," Seth repeats, standing there with wide eyes that refuse to blink. "Just—don't."

He rubs his nose and wipes his eyes and heads out of the bathroom. I stay behind, looking at the drops of red on the white floor and the white sink. Then I look at myself in the mirror and wish the guy I'm staring at could figure out how to help those in his life who really need it.

# 6

I'm staring up at the high ceiling when all around me I hear loud noises. Screams. Wailing and shrieks. I turn and feel a hand grip my arm.

Marvel's next to me. I smother her with my arms and my body to protect her.

I feel the world shaking and wonder what's happening and why I can't breathe. Underneath me Marvel's trembling and coughing but I can tell one very important thing.

She's alive.

Crumbling, violent explosions with the world swallowing itself, and yet she's alive. She's okay.

For now.

I wake up clutching my pillow. It's ridiculous, really, that I've become like a series of trailers for disaster movies. I've never dreamt so much in my life as I have this past year.

But if nightmares are the price for having Marvel in my life, so be it.

I get showered and dressed and am grabbing

breakfast when Mom comes into the kitchen. She looks like a sleepwalker.

"You're all dressed up."

I'm only wearing khakis with a button-down shirt. But yeah, I guess she's right, especially for a Sunday morning.

"I'm going to church."

"With Marvel?" She pours herself a cup of the coffee I made.

"With Harry and his family." Harry is my boss, the owner of Fascination Street Records.

Mom turns and looks at me. "Well, that's nice."

"That I'm going?"

"That they asked you to."

"I'm eating lunch with them too."

She laughs in a not-so-funny way. "It'll be better than what you'd get here."

"I'm sure they wouldn't mind if you came along."

Mom sits down at the table next to me. Her face looks like it's being tugged down by life. "I'm not in the mood to talk to him."

"Harry?"

"No. God."

Mom's rarely mentioned God to me. In fact, I don't think we've ever had a conversation about God and faith. Not in any specific way.

"Why?"

"I'm not someone who spends a lot of time thinking about God. We haven't gone to church much. I thought it would be a good idea with you three boys. We tried some when you were all younger. But I've prayed for your father over the years and I've gotten nothing. Nothing but this."

"Maybe it's good that Dad's gone."

"But nobody knows where he is. And that means he could show up at the house anytime. Or show up in a morgue looking blue. *That's* not an answer to any kind of prayer I've prayed."

I wonder if God's answered my unspoken prayers. I wonder if he's given me one of the things I wanted the most: for Dad to be gone. I'm not about to tell Mom my thoughts. I think she's still angry at me for standing up for my brother and attacking my father. Maybe she's angry at me for causing her to call the cops and causing Dad to disappear. Whatever it might be, I don't need to add to the list.

I can't think of anything to say except that I need to get going.

"Well—if you see or hear from God, tell him I'm still waiting for some answers," she says.

I think about Marvel.

*I am too, Mom. I am too.*

# 7

Sarah Reeves looks like she's accustomed to having three boys hanging on her, and at the same time tackling each other and breaking things in their path. Harry introduces me quickly to the boys, and I focus hard to remember their names. Scott is the oldest, a tall kid about to turn eight but looks like he could be ten. Mark is five and in kindergarten and doesn't talk much. The baby is Ben, who just turned three and looks like a mini terror.

Watching what these parents have to put up with makes me appreciate mine a little more. Well, at least my mother.

"Lunch is almost ready," Sarah says from the kitchen.

Harry and I are on the couches in the family room watching the Blackhawks. They're up 2–1, and I can tell Harry's into it.

"Do the boys like hockey?" I ask.

"Yeah. Hey, Scott, knock it off!"

The eldest son shrugs and lets go of his youngest brother's jaw. "Ben's biting me," he whines.

"Stop being a brat then."

Harry glances at me and shakes his head. "They're actually being halfway decent today."

We both laugh. I can't imagine what it would be like to have three children. Especially three boys. But then again, I know I'd do a better job than some fathers of the world. Some MIA fathers who like to beat up on their eldest sons.

"You a Hawks fan?" Harry asks.

"No. I mean, they're fine. It's just—my father is into all these sports. And it kinda turned me against it."

Harry turns down the volume a bit. The boys wander into the other room so we can actually hear ourselves talk.

"My father liked fishing," Harry says. "And I hate it. I mean—he would drag me out on the water so early in the morning on this little lake in Michigan, and I'd just sit there freezing, thinking a thousand different things. We never talked."

"Did you catch a lot of fish?" I ask.

"Does it matter? I don't like how they taste. I think I'm scarred by sitting in that boat doing nothing but wishing I could be anywhere else. Wishing he'd just reach out a little and share what he was thinking."

I don't say much, and maybe Harry thinks of my situation.

"I shouldn't complain," he adds. "My dad loved me. Fishing was one way he felt like he could bond with me, but heaven forbid he'd actually talk to me. Or express an emotion. But I think that was just his age and generation."

I want to say, *At least he didn't bash your head with a vodka bottle.*

"Any news on your father?" Harry asks.

The daily ritual of questions. *Where's your father? Where's Carlos? Where's Santa Claus? Where's the Grim Reaper?*

"No," I say.

The Hawks score, and our conversation shifts to something else. It's easy to do that today. There are a million things that can take our attention away from the few things that matter. But I don't want to talk about Dad or about missing people or about how much I fear when we're in our home late at night.

When a commercial comes, Harry faces me again.

"You know something? My thought when it comes to my father? Or really anybody in this life? It sorta boils down to one thing."

He pauses for a moment, and I wait to hear what he's thinking. Harry looks away, perhaps trying to figure out what exactly to say, perhaps just reflecting on it himself.

"Anytime I feel like I've been wronged by someone—in my past or even some jerk cutting me off in traffic—I try to imagine what God might feel like every time I wrong him. You know? I just know that I have to give grace to others because, man . . . God's given so much to me."

I nod, looking down at the ground, hearing his words but still not connecting.

Harry gives me a heartfelt look. "You know—anything you need, Brandon. You know . . ."

"Yeah," I say.

I haven't worked as many hours lately. That's probably a combination of Harry not needing me as much and Marvel no longer being there to work alongside. Things will get busier as spring approaches, Harry has told me, and then it gets really busy heading into Record Store Day, which is usually a Saturday in April.

At the dinner table—or at least the idea of a dinner table since the three boys sit, then stand, then run around, then are forced to sit again—Harry gives thanks for the food and then Sarah asks me what I thought of church.

"It was good," I say. "Smaller than I thought it'd be."

The church is named Oasis and it's in the middle of Aurora. Harry told me that it ministers to a lot of people who are just beginning to rebuild their lives after things like being in prison or having an addiction. I can't help but think of my father when he says that, but I know it would take a miracle like Moses parting the Red Sea to get my father into any church.

"They preach the gospel," Harry says. "It's good to go somewhere and not be lost in the crowd. We've been to some churches that were so big it was easy to be just in the masses."

"There are good people there," Sarah says.

I've met Harry's wife before, but always while she's with the kids. She always seems half distracted. I wonder if my mom was that way when my brothers and I were little, then realize that of course she was.

"Do you have a church you regularly attend?" Sarah asks.

"No. Not really. I've gone to a Bible church with my girlf—well, with a girl."

Sarah looks at Harry, and they both smile.

"Brandon has a girl he's been chasing since the start of summer."

"Chasing, huh," Sarah says.

"Not chasing," I say. "Just—it's complicated."

Harry leans over to me and pretends to whisper. "Women are all complicated. I keep telling you that."

His wife disagrees. "We're not complicated." She wipes her mouth with a napkin. "We're just stronger and brighter and better-looking."

Harry shrugs. His hair is a bit wilder than usual and he hasn't shaved in a while. "I can't argue with that."

For a while there, in these simple moments full of loud outbreaks and cries and laughter from the three boys, I feel like I'm in a normal story. Like I'm part of something good, something that can make me a better person. I want to just stay here for a long time, like maybe another year. I don't want to go back home.

After lunch we watch the Blackhawks a while longer, and then I tell Harry I need to leave.

"You sure?" he asks. Then he glances around and adds, "Wanna take me?"

"You have a nice family," I say.

"I know. I'm blessed. I have to remind myself of that. I have three healthy boys and a wonderful wife. Would be nice to have a little more job security, but we can't have everything, can we?"

"Probably not."

He shifts on the couch and studies me for a moment. "You know, Brandon. The best thing to do—the *only* thing to do sometimes—is pray. We just pray and pray a little more, and then we pray again. I know God hears us."

"Does he answer?" I ask.

Harry nods. "Always. Sometimes even his silence is an answer. Know that. But I also believe there are seasons in this life. And sometimes it's hard to transition from one season to another. I'm currently wondering—maybe fighting that myself."

I don't quite understand what he's saying. "Seasons?"

"God doesn't necessarily want us to be *happy*. He wants us to be more like himself. So he does everything he can to make that happen."

"So that means—what?" I ask. "Like being more holy or something?"

"No. I think it's a lot of things. God continues to mold and shape us when we believe in him."

I think of myself as a round and pudgy ball of Play-Doh. That's pretty much how I look, with soccer season in the distant past.

"You know, Brandon, you're not far from a different season in college."

"Don't remind me," I say.

We talk about college and about my lack of interest in it. I don't want to think about a different season right now. I just want to figure how to make it to my high school graduation. With Marvel at my side. And my father far, far away.

Maybe Harry understands that too. Surely he can tell how I feel about my father. Before I head back home, he leaves me with another thought.

"Do you know the story of Rahab in the Bible?" he asks.

I shake my head. I don't need to tell him that I don't really know a lot about the Bible.

"It's a story from the Old Testament. From the book of Joshua. Rahab was a woman who helped the Israelites out. She hid some spies in this gated city called Jericho.

You know—you've heard about the walls of Jericho coming down?"

I nod but I'm not really sure. I think that maybe I heard about that in a song, like a Kanye West song or something, and then I wonder how in the world a Bible story got me thinking about a rapper.

"So this Rahab was a prostitute, but God used her to help his people out," Harry says. "She actually turns out to be an ancestor of Jesus. Think about that. It makes me think—it makes me *believe*—that God's love is powerful enough to get over any wall. He can open anyone's heart and find them. And—thankfully for all of us—forgive them."

# 8

We stand outside overlooking the half-frozen river while icy snowflakes hit our faces and quickly melt away. The coffee we're sipping makes us a little warmer.

"We can go in," I tell her.

"I've been in a long time. It's nice to be outside."

"Yeah. Unless you get frostbite."

"Maybe you just have to stand a little closer," Marvel says with a smile.

She's got her black wool cap on with strands of dark hair sneaking out. I put my coffee on the stone wall of the bridge and put my arms around her.

Marvel moves her head back. "Whoa, now. I only said stand a little closer."

"I am."

She grins up at me. I love seeing joy in her expression.

"Can I just stay with you?" I ask.

"We have school tomorrow."

"Doesn't matter."

"You have a job. I have a place to hide from my crazy uncle."

"I just don't want to leave you. At all. Ever."

She shakes her head. I glance at the full lips I really, really want to kiss.

"You get a bit full of ideas when you get this close," she says.

"You make me get this way."

"Is it the new scarf?"

I shake my head and give her that look. There was a time when I gave her that look and she didn't understand it. It's the kind of look all guys in high school have—well, that every male over fourteen has—and I've been carrying it around on my face for a while. She understands it now.

*It's not the scarf—it's called desire and it fills me morning, noon, and night.*

She gives me that look. It's one she's been giving me for a while too. It's a combination of amusement and regret and hesitation. I think this look is covering up the same look I have, because I see it start to leak out sometimes.

I don't make a big deal of this moment. It happens often, it'll happen again. All I can do is move on. That or jump into the river.

"You know that London Grammar album you told me about?" I ask.

She nods.

"'I don't have a soul like you,'" I quote. "'The only one I have is the one I stole from you.'"

"Maybe I gave it to you," Marvel says.

The hesitating, hold-on-there look suddenly vanishes, and

I see my longing mirrored on her face. Then she pulls me toward her and kisses me while the wind and the flurries keep breathing down our necks.

I no longer wonder if someone is watching us. Or chasing us. Or scheming to do something to us.

I feel a little like we're the last two people on the planet. And that's okay.

Soon reality will strike and my feet will be back down on the sidewalk and she'll hand me back my heart and soul. Even if I don't want to take them.

On my way back from dropping Marvel off, with the snow continuing to fall and the sky now dark, I find myself thinking of Devon. It's like noticing this big hole in my side. I can cover it up with noise and busyness. But it never goes away.

I haven't seen Devon's parents. The few times I've called they've been busy, either just ready to leave their house or working on something or about to receive guests. I think I remind them too much of their dead son. And that's the last thing I want to do, to be some kind of grim snapshot they want to toss into the Fox River and watch float away.

The snow seems to pick up as I drive. It's nice to be in a white blanket, knowing nobody is watching or following me.

*Well, nobody except God.*

"Are you there?" I say out loud.

Of course I don't hear him. Only people like Moses and Marvel get to hear the voice of God talking to them.

*Maybe you don't want to hear from God. Maybe you're scared of what he would say.*

So I do what the pastor and Harry said. I try to talk to this

God who's out there somewhere, maybe seeing me and maybe hearing me.

"God, what do you want out of my life? What am I supposed to do?"

I ask this, thinking of Marvel.

"Do you really want me to save her? Or save someone else?"

I have more questions than requests. And it feels weird to talk to the same God that all those Bible people used to talk to.

*Will he ever talk to me?*

I'd love to see some kind of message on a church sign or maybe one of those changing electronic billboards.

Brandon Jeffrey, you are meant to meet Marvel in the coffee shop at 8:34 Tuesday morning to save her from death and destruction.

Instead the night passes by without even a wave or a smile from God.

"Protect her," I say.

I don't really care much about myself. I do, of course, as every person does in a self-preserving sort of way. But with my father still out there and Uncle Carlos . . .

"Show me something, God. Please. Show me an answer. Open some door or show me some kind of road to go down."

I'm focused on the sky as I talk and suddenly feel the whole car vibrate and jerk. I look in the rearview mirror and see that I've gone through a massive pothole. It nearly blasted out my front left tire.

It reminds me of the time Devon and I drove over a cat many, many lives ago.

I stop the car to make sure the tire is okay. For a while I stand outside the car and look back up at the sky. Was this a sign or merely my fault for looking up instead of looking straight ahead?

Maybe it's good to pray, but it's also good to keep an eye out for craters in the road.

# 9

I spot Marvel and smile at her, but she doesn't smile back. And something in me wonders if I'll ever see Marvel's smile again, the Marvel I once knew, the Marvel before everything.

*Hold on, wait; she's not smiling but why?*

Then I see a casket and wonder if we're back at my elderly cousin Earl's funeral. Or maybe Devon's funeral. So many deaths in such a short time.

But this is different.

This is somehow worse.

*It can't be.*

I want to move away. This isn't real, I feel it. Marvel's not real. I can tell.

She shakes her head, wipes tears, brushes back her dark hair, leans over to look at the ground. I want to put my arm around her but I can't.

I look around and see so many people.

Whoever died was important. Someone important. Something big. Something . . .

"It was supposed to be me," she whispers.

"Stop it."

"Something went wrong. Something changed. I don't know why. I'm not meant to still be here."

But I shake my head and say no. I tell her no and tell this dream no and tell the storyteller no no no. I say wake up. Wake up now, Brandon. WAKE UP.

So I do. Not in some gasp. Not in a sweat. Just opening my eyes and finding it's 3:24 a.m.

Another dream. So real. So wrong. So eerie.

*But Marvel's there and that's all that matters.*

Or so I tell myself. But is that right? Is that really what matters?

I stay up for a long time thinking about it.

When the morning arrives, my mom has to wake me up because I spent half the night trying not to fall back asleep. I slip on the first pair of jeans I see on the floor and the first random shirt I find in my dresser. I like the fact that I spend zero time in my life thinking about fashion. I prefer to see others doing that. Well, let's say I prefer seeing Marvel do that.

I want to text her but she beats me to it, letting me know that she's posted something new on her blog. She says it was inspired by the song I mentioned last night. I just smile.

**Aren't your followers supposed to be notified about your posts?** I write to her.

**You're my only follower, and this is me notifying you.**

I want to think of something clever to say in return but I have nothing this morning.

After a moment she texts, **I'll see you soon. Don't be late.**

I go to her blog on my phone and scroll to find the newest posting.

### STAY AWAKE

There is a bridge and I think I belong there

I think my steps will cross it soon enough

I know your belief and your persistence and your feisty spirit all say no, but I continue to see it

So just stay there.

Be there.

Take my hand and guide me as far as you can.

Don't forget where you've gone and how far we've come and where we're going

The world watches but doesn't truly pay attention

Take your heart and come and find me

That's all I ask when I'm gone

I think I'll still be there. Somewhere out there.

I don't know what it looks like but I believe.

I believe that I'll still be there

In the shadowy still of night

In the glowing sun of the morning

I believe I'll follow you on sidewalks and street corners

I think I'll remind you of how you belong to me

> I don't want to hover or harass but I do think I'll hear you
>
> I think I'll warm over your soul in some kind of way
>
> And I think you'll somehow know
>
> Don't run away but stand still as the heavens seep down
>
> Don't fear but stand strong as the world beats you down
>
> Don't forget but always remember how much I love you
>
> Like now
>
> Like the sun remembers
>
> Like the air you breathe
>
> Like the shadow that sees
>
> Stay awake while the dark despair sings its lullabies to the world
>
> Stay awake to stay strong
>
> And wait for the day we can meet at the first tree that grows inside the golden gates
>
> Where you can tell me everything you saw along the way

I think of the dream I had last night. Her blog is a reminder—no, make that an order—to stay strong and stay awake and make sure Marvel doesn't find that bridge she's talking about. Not yet. Not now.

I don't want to run and I don't want to fear, and I do not want to see her cross over to anywhere unless I'm holding her hand and crossing with her.

# 10

Lee Fleisher is an older guy who shows up at Fascination Street at least once a week. He's mentioned my helping with yardwork or snow removal in the past, and I always said I'd be happy to help out, so when he calls and asks me to come by after school, I feel obligated to go. I wonder if he'll be wearing colorful beach shorts even in the dead of winter.

Lee lives in the nearby town of Geneva, so after school lets out, I put his address in my phone's GPS and drive to the house. My shovel's in my backseat, but he said he has a snowblower. I wonder how long his driveway happens to be and if his snowblower will be working.

The house is on a corner lot on top of a hill—which is unusual, since most of northern Illinois is flat. Dense pine trees hide the house, so I can't tell from the road if it's large or not. But there's a driveway on either side of the house, meaning if I *don't* get to use a snowblower I'm in serious trouble.

I park on the curb and make tracks through the six-inch-deep snow. The sun has already checked out behind the mass of clouds above me. The blinds are closed and I don't see any lights on inside as I ring the doorbell. I wait, then knock on the door, wait, then ring again.

After ten or fifteen minutes I get the feeling that Mr. Fleisher isn't here. So I walk around the driveway, which seems to curve all the way around his property. A garage door happens to be open, but instead of a car sitting inside I see a red snowblower.

"Hello? Mr. Fleisher?"

I feel very cold, in spite of my thick winter coat and hat and gloves.

"Anybody here?"

I wonder if I'm just supposed to do the job without talking. But Mr. Fleisher loves to talk. I can't imagine his missing a chance to do so. Maybe his wife is inside and doesn't want to be bothered.

A gust of wind blasts through me sideways and I glance at the long driveway heading down the hill. The pine trees shake and the snow whips around as if it's dancing, and suddenly I feel something grabbing at me. Nothing I can see, but just a feeling. Like I'm being watched. Like I'm in danger. Yet there are no cars on the street, nobody hiding behind the trees, nobody I can see anywhere.

The snowblower waits near the back of the garage.

I blink and see darkness all around me. A cold glove smelling like gasoline covers my face. I can't move and I start to black out, and the last thing I see is the garage door shutting.

Then I shake my head and blink and see the half-light of the day. I'm still standing on the driveway, feeling a sinking sort of sickness inside. The garage door is still open.

"Mr. Fleisher?" I call out again.

I realize that I didn't tell anybody I was coming here. Not my mom. Or my brothers. Not even Marvel.

I feel dizzy and aching, as though I just worked out for an hour. I think about what I ate for lunch; I wonder if one of my brothers passed along the flu, if the cold is getting to me.

But everything tells me it's something else.

Someone else.

I glance at the snowblower I'm supposed to be using. I don't know why, but something doesn't seem right.

So I walk back down the driveway. I'm freaked out but not sure why.

When I get to the car, I look up at the house. I wonder if someone is inside, staring out at me.

Maybe I've just gotten a little too used to bad people waiting for me behind closed doors.

Maybe there's something else happening to me, something I don't understand. Something that very much has to do with Marvel and what's happening to her.

# 11

"Where do you think Dad is?"

The three of us are playing Xbox when Carter's comment comes out of nowhere. Maybe it's because we're killing zombies that he thinks of our father?

"Hopefully he drowned in the Fox River," Alex says.

"Shut up," I tell him.

We all might dislike our father. *Hate* might even be an appropriate word. But nobody should wish death on anybody.

"Just keeping it real," he says.

I knock him on the back of his head. "How about not 'keepin' it real.' And don't start trying to sound tough or anything. Okay?"

Alex curses at me. I just shake my head.

"What's wrong with you?" I ask.

"What's wrong with *you*? Sticking up for a guy who likes to beat you up."

"I'm not sticking up for anybody. He's our father, you know."

"Yeah, I know it."

Alex sounds and looks older than he ever has. I understand his anger—I *share* his anger—but I hate seeing it in my brother.

"You think he's still alive?" Carter asks.

He still sounds like the baby. I have a feeling that even when he's grown and married with kids, to me Carter will always be a kid.

"Yeah," I say.

"Really?"

"Sure. Why not?"

"Then why doesn't he come back?"

"'Cause he's afraid of being arrested, which he will be if he comes back," Alex says.

"Really?"

I nod at Carter. "Yeah. Afraid so."

"Afraid?" Alex asks. "What you should be afraid of is Dad coming back with a gun or a knife."

"He won't," I say.

But I've had the same thoughts myself.

"You don't know *what* he'll do."

"Just chill," I tell Alex.

"Maybe you're just a little too 'chilled.'"

I pause the game and look at Alex.

"What?" he asks.

"Hating him isn't going to change what he did."

Alex seems to grit his teeth as he stares at the television and doesn't even look at me.

"I can hate whoever I want to," he says.

Rage on one brother's face. Fear and confusion on the other's. It's not a pleasant picture.

"If either of you sees Dad, you tell me," I say. "You got it? Call me. Text me. The second you see him."

"I'm gonna call the cops," Alex says.

I can't argue with that decision. It really is the smartest.

I picture the angry man who pounded a vodka bottle against my forehead.

Then I picture myself sinking deep in the waters of Lake Michigan.

*If God can pull me out and help me, then maybe I can do the same for Dad.*

I'm not trying to be holy or good or anything like that. But it's my father. And I gotta stop hating him. Because hate sure doesn't look good.

"You guys think he'll always drink?" Carter asks after the game resumes.

"Yes," Alex says.

"Maybe not," I say. "People can change."

"No, they can't. There's no way Dad's gonna change."

I'm not sure what to say. Part of me agrees, believes that someone like my father or Marvel's uncle or the evil people out there won't ever change. But maybe God would have something different to say about that.

"Wonder if we'll end up like that," Carter says.

"Like what?" Alex says in an angry tone.

"Having problems, you know. With the drinking. They say it runs in the family."

"I'll never get drunk like that," Alex says. "Never."

Carter doesn't say anything and neither do I. My middle

brother's anger and defiance are natural, and I get it. But I also know that sometimes you say something's not gonna happen and it does. I think again of Devon and how dismissive I was and how I didn't pay full attention.

*How you failed him.*

"You two just be careful," I tell them.

"With Dad?"

"With everything. Okay? There are bad people out there."

"Like Marvel's uncle?" Carter asks.

They know the story just like everybody else.

"Yeah."

That's all I say.

I wish I could be both of their shadows the same way I'm trying to look after Marvel. But I can't. Eventually they have to open the door and step outside and encounter whatever the world might bring them.

I just pray that it won't be something purely evil. I've seen what that looks like. And I barely survived.

# 12

I'm driving home from school when I spot a police car in our driveway. For a second I think about turning around and driving away. Not because I did something wrong. It's just I'm not in a mood to try to set something right.

Instead, I park the Honda and get out. My legs feel rubbery and heavy, and I move at about a third of my usual speed. When I get inside, I find Sergeant Mike Harden talking to my mom.

"Did you find Dad?" I blurt without waiting to be spoken to.

"No," Mom says.

"Hello, Brandon."

I say hi to Harden.

"Everything going okay?" he asks.

"Yeah. What happened?"

"Nothing," Mom tells me. "Everything's okay."

"I've been telling your mother that we checked out the old Stonehill Armory."

I don't respond, because I have no idea what the Stonehill Armory is or why he's telling me this.

"The warehouse on Rush Street. With the smokestack. The one you reported to us when we questioned you."

*Aha.*

"Yeah, okay."

"It's empty. Nothing's in there. Nada. No sign of anybody having been there, either."

"There weren't people," I say. "There was like some kind of big brick oven."

Sergeant Harden shakes his head. The light reflects on his scalp underneath the buzz haircut. "Whatever you might have seen is no longer there."

"Maybe they didn't want it to be seen," I say.

He nods, though he doesn't necessarily look like he's believing me.

"I swear I saw something in there."

He gives me a slow, serious stare. "You might have seen something. We also interviewed Otis Sykes."

"And?"

Mom gives me a stern look as if I did something wrong.

"What?" I ask.

"You need to stay away from Otis. Okay?"

What's she talking about?

"What? Why?"

"Because he issued a restraining order," she says.

I look at her and then at the sergeant. "A what? For who?"

"For you, Brandon."

"Are you serious?"

The expression on the officer's face confirms it. "Yes,

unfortunately, I am. But listen—the guy is a mean old man, and for some reason you've really pissed him off. But all you have to do is stay away from him."

"I've never bothered him. I've never done a thing. He's got something to do with Marvel's uncle and Devon's death. I know he does. Marvel's uncle practically told me so."

"There's nothing to prove that connection, Brandon. There's nothing we can do against Otis. Seriously, you don't want to mess with him. Filing a restraint is just his warning shot."

"But you think he's innocent?" I shout.

"No. But a murderer? I don't think so. Otis isn't the killer around here."

"He might be hiding the killer."

The officer walks over to me and puts a hand on my shoulder. "Brandon—you know the truth now. We know the truth. I'm sorry about your friend. And we're doing everything we can to find Carlos. You just keep safe, okay? And please—do not go near Otis. Do not have anything to do with the old guy. Okay?"

I give him an unconvincing nod.

"Brandon?"

"Okay."

"We're going to find Carlos," he tells us. "I promise you we will. You just stay safe."

"Keep Marvel safe," I say.

That's all I'm really worried about.

And something keeps telling me that nobody can promise me that.

# 13

It's the first week of March and the day is surprisingly warm. I'm driving Marvel to school because her aunt had to be somewhere early, so we approach from the opposite direction than usual. Maybe that's why I see things I've never bothered to notice before. They stand out to me on this early Monday morning.

Kids walking to school. A group of students I don't know. Others walking by themselves. Some with hoods covering their heads. Some with earbuds in, their faces down in another world. Girls in black. Guys laughing with each other. Everybody walking down the sidewalk toward Appleton High.

I see the mothers driving their kids to school. Then there are the students driving. Some faces I recognize. Some cars I know.

We're all heading to this place where we spend a majority of our days. Not because we want to. We're stuck here together and forced to live and breathe and eat and learn together. Side by side.

"What are you thinking about?" Marvel asks.

We're almost to the school parking lot, and I'm far more quiet than usual.

"Just school," I say.

"What about school?"

"It'll be nice not to have to go to school one day," I tell her.

I don't mean anything by my comment. But I see the serious look fall on her face like a lone cloud suddenly covering the sun.

"Don't," I tell her.

"I'm not."

"Don't go there," I order.

"I'm not going anywhere."

"Anytime I talk about the future you go there. To that place."

She looks out her window, away from me.

"Marvel?"

"What?"

"You know you do that. Every time I make a comment like that—anything to do with a future 'one day'—I'm always, always thinking that you're there too. You know that."

She nods.

"Then what's wrong?" I ask.

"I'd like to know too, Brandon."

"Like to know what?"

"What it would be like to not have school. To move on. To not have this weight around my soul."

I don't have to ask what the weight is or how heavy it happens to be.

"Can I carry some of it?" I ask instead.

"You do. Every day. And it's getting lighter."

I touch my arm. "Good, because you know how buff I am. I can lift whatever weight I need to."

This makes her laugh, of course.

We pull into the parking lot, ready for another day at high school. Both of us ready to try to carry that collective weight that never seems to go away.

School is different without Devon. Some days I feel it more than others.

My locker is lonelier without Devon coming up to me, peering in to comment on how messy I am. Sharing some story or random thought. Just *being* there.

Today there's no shadow by my locker, no quirky smile, no silly tale I would only halfway listen to.

*You'd listen now if he were around.*

I'd probably do a lot of things if Devon were around.

I see everybody pass me by in slow motion as if somehow I'm walking around in some kind of strange bubble. And maybe I am. Maybe Devon's death is going to be like some kind of weird shadow hanging around for the rest of my life.

*If it's like this with Devon, what would it be like if—?*

I stop and try to strangle the thought out of my mind.

I don't want to go there. Again. Death. Sadness. Separation. I don't want to think of this *again* when it comes to Marvel.

I can feel the anger inside of me, and it makes everybody else around me disappear.

There's only one person I can direct this anger toward. God, the one who knows about everything and sees everything and *allows* all the things that happen. But I know I can't be angry at him. I shouldn't.

Still it's there, like the absence of Devon, like the silence surrounding me, like the shadows seeming to follow my every step.

The assembly in the fine arts theater at the west end of the high school is rare. I can only remember a few others in my nearly four years at Appleton High. The building is relatively new, and the theater is bursting at the seams when the entire school population congregates. They say it seats twelve hundred, but looking around, I see some kids standing in the aisles and near the back of the auditorium.

I'm sitting with Marvel and the guys in the middle mezzanine section. Since we were all summoned over the PA during the period after lunch, there wasn't any rhyme or reason to the way students filed in the two entrances. It feels like a pep rally, except we usually have those in the gym.

"What do you think this is about?" I ask Frankie, who sits on my left.

"Nothing sports-related. I know that."

"Maybe it has something to do with Devon," Marvel whispers.

I nod. I glance around but don't pay attention to anybody. It seems like another life when people like my ex-girlfriend Taryn and Greg and others annoyed me. When I actually thought about them. Now there are bigger and darker things on my mind.

Eventually the principal, Mr. Andersen, shows up onstage and tries to calm everybody down. Most of the students cooperate.

"I know this is a bit unusual, but I tell our staff that we need to use this theater more often, even if it's a bit crowded. There are still empty seats. If those of you who have seats will move to the center of the rows we can get more people seated. That'd be great."

This takes a lot longer than it probably should, and of course there are still students without seats. Mr. Andersen just lets it go.

"All of us are aware of the difficult year that our school is having. That our town is having. I hope that you are still being careful, still staying in groups, and still staying *aware* of what's going on around you. Once again, we encourage you to let your parents or your teachers or any adult in your life know if you see anything strange or suspicious. We're doing everything possible to keep all of you safe."

He looks over to one side of the stage, and a tall, bald-headed man walks out and stands next to him.

"This is Mr. Culsum," the principal says. "He's going to speak to us twice, today and again in several weeks, about a very important subject. Bullying. Please listen to what he has to say."

The guy begins talking in a strange, high-pitched voice. He's got a microphone wired to him and he starts a stand-up routine. But little by little, the jokes begin to make more students laugh. He does impressions—great ones. Arnold

Schwarzenegger. President Obama. Christopher Walken, who I only know from *Saturday Night Live*. But the best is Jim Carrey. This gets everybody howling. But he's talking about kids who are bullied, and of course this is his way to get all of us listening for when he starts to make his points.

Mr. Culsum stresses the selfish nature of bullying and how insecurity usually breeds it. He spends a while talking about cyberbullying too. I glance around the crowd to see if I can spot my ex-girlfriend or maybe the football team. Thankfully I can't. But I hope they're listening.

I wonder what Seth is thinking.

The guy ends with a few more classic impressions, then the principal comes out and thanks him before sending us off to our next class.

It takes everybody a while to file out of the theater. I look over at Marvel.

"What are you thinking?" I ask.

"Nothing."

But I can tell something's bothering her. Maybe she's thinking about Devon again. Or just the whole drama of the past year with the football stud Greg bullying the oddball Seth, leading to a lot of bad stuff including Frankie's broken arm.

It's another reminder that I can't wait until graduation day. I hope to be there in a robe and hat holding Marvel's hand and breathing a really awesome sigh of relief.

# 14

Sometimes you need to run fast to escape the shadows. So that evening, with nothing planned and nobody telling us what to do, Marvel and I decide to escape. She asks for a little time to get ready. I'm not sure where we'll go, but I head over to pick her up a little after six. I don't see any police nearby as I drive up to the curb, but then again they're not trying to be seen.

Marvel skips out the front door and waves at me. She's wearing a long blue-and-black floral skirt with a dark sweater and a massive belt between the two. Her hair is tucked under a fashionable black knit cap, and her long, flowing sweater-jacket looks great with her tall boots.

"Guess how much this outfit cost me," she says as she climbs into my Honda.

I shake my head as I inhale the scent of strawberries. Even in the chill of winter this girl is alive with springtime.

"Ten bucks. Mostly on the boots. The lady at the thrift store gave me the jacket and belt *free*."

Before I can reply, she gives me a kiss on my cheek.

"So where are we going?" I ask.

I think about some of the past places we've gone when we've slipped away. Downtown Chicago, where we watched an outdoor party hidden between buildings. A nursing home, where we hung out in the lobby while my mom visited her elderly cousin Earl. The indoor shopping mall we practically had to ourselves during a snowstorm. Or outside under the sky, watching the moon nod off above us.

"Somewhere very close," Marvel says. "You get to save gas money. Just drive straight ahead. I'll tell you where to go."

In ten minutes she directs me to a parking garage close to the casino in downtown Aurora.

"So are we going to hit the slots or the roulette wheel?" I joke.

Well, make that half joke, because Marvel always seems to surprise me.

"Very funny," she says. "If I'm going to take a gamble with my money, I'll give it to some homeless person."

It takes me a moment to figure out why that would be a gamble. She only laughs.

She guides me to the sidewalk and across the street to the Paramount Theatre.

"It's Classic Movie Monday," she says as we walk into the old ornate building. "Don't look at the sign over there." She takes my hand and pulls me the other way. "I want it to be a surprise."

If it's a classic, I figure the movie has to be fairly old. And if Marvel chose it, I'm betting it's going to be a love story.

There are ushers at the entrance and near the aisles. The theater is massive and spectacular and has a warm, crimson glow. Marvel guides me to the middle of the center row of seats. There are patches of people here and there, but it's nowhere near full.

"I've never been here," I say. "I didn't realize it was this nice."

"It's amazing what's right behind you if you simply turn around and notice. So take a guess what we're seeing."

"Some romance. Maybe romantic comedy."

She just smiles.

"You want me to guess a real film?" I ask.

"Yep."

My hand rests with hers on her lap. She's taken off her cap but somehow her hair still looks perfect. The dark eyes just watch me.

"You know I don't really know films."

"You gotta guess," she says. "Just one."

I honestly can't think of any older films. Finally I remember a title. "*When Harry Met Sally*?"

She tightens her full lips and shakes her head. "Not even close."

The theater goes dark and the film starts. Right away I can tell it's old. Like *decades* old. Two British guys are talking about something and I'm half watching the screen and then watching Marvel. Then I catch the word "oh-oh-seven."

"Is this a Bond movie?" I whisper.

"Shhhh."

Miss Moneypenny appears, then the famous theme song plays over a car driving. Still I don't recognize the movie.

"Is this a Sean Connery one?" I ask.

"Be quiet," Marvel says playfully.

GLORY

All I can see is some guy smoking and driving a car while following a woman to the beach. When she suddenly starts walking into the ocean with its rushing waves, as if she wants to kill herself or something, the mysterious smoking guy drives down to the sand and then goes to save her. Finally the camera shows his face and he introduces himself as "Bond, James Bond" . . . but it's a Bond I've never seen.

"Who is that?" I ask Marvel.

"No commentary."

I can't believe Marvel brought me to a Bond film. Seriously.

There's a fight sequence and then the girl gets away. Cue the opening sequence with the profiles of naked ladies swimming and floating around while scenes from previous James Bond films glide down the scene. The movie is called *On Her Majesty's Secret Service*, a very un-Bond-sounding title. *Goldfinger* and *Moonraker* and *GoldenEye*—those are what 007 movies should sound like. Then I see the name of the actor.

"Who is George Lazenby?" I whisper.

"Love the name."

"Did you know this was playing?" I ask her while the theme song blares with trumpets and horns.

"Any time I hear of James Bond I think of you," Marvel tells me.

"Because I'm so suave and debonair, right?"

"No. Because of Adele's theme song."

July Fourth. Watching fireworks and hearing "Skyfall." Ah, yes. I'll never forget.

"But who is this guy?" I ask her again.

It turns out that this is unlike any Bond movie I've ever seen. Sean Connery was so alpha male cool. This guy is kinda geeky cool. He's sort of a hipster Bond, though that term was surely not in use back when this was made. Probably in the . . .

"Is this a seventies film?" I ask.

Of course it is. Seventies all the time every time. That's how it goes with Marvel.

"Sixty-nine," she whispers. "Close enough. Now hush and watch."

The film starts off as more of a love story than anything else, with Bond chasing Tracy, the woman he rescued, and then getting an offer from her criminal-of-sorts father to marry her simply to keep her out of trouble. A sappy song plays behind a romantic montage.

Marvel is still holding my hand, and I look over at her. She grins at me. I still don't know if she's seen this movie before or not.

A guy with a familiar low, raspy voice starts singing, "We have all the time in the world." The couple is walking and petting a cat.

*They're petting a cat. What in the world has happened to James Bond?*

Then they're shopping and running on a beach playing tag and riding horses and looking at wedding rings and what the heck is going on here?

Marvel leans over on my shoulder. "That's Louis Armstrong singing."

I nod. Again, I'm lost. I'm thinking that maybe this is supposed to be a moment—like the kind we shared on July

Fourth with Adele—but I can't get over Hipster Bond going all Nicholas Sparks on us. And Louis Armstrong? I'm thinking of Neil Armstrong on the moon or Lance Armstrong on his bike.

"He sang 'What a Wonderful World,'" she tells me.

"Oh yeah. That's where I've heard him."

There's another plotline, something about a coat of arms and trying to get at the bad guy, but I still don't get it. Eventually Bond heads up into the Swiss Alps to go undercover as a nerdy genealogist researching coats of arms. As they show scenes of him flying over the beautiful mountains, Marvel rests her head on my shoulder. I see her starting to drift off. Chances are I might too.

Bond goes back to his Bond ways up at the chalet on top of a mountain, where he's surrounded by all these exotic ladies who fall all over him. I guess he's not *that* into the cat lady he was dating. Or maybe that's just what he has to do for Her Majesty's Secret Service.

Eventually his true identity gets found out. I mean—no genealogist has ever seduced so many good-looking ladies. He's imprisoned, then escapes on skis in a cool sequence with his even cooler theme song playing again. His girlfriend/love-of-his-life-unless-he's-in-a-Swiss-chalet-with-a-dozen-models saves his life and they hide out. Then they ski again and then get caught in an avalanche, and Tracy gets taken.

By this time Marvel's off to dreamland. Maybe because she's seen this film before, but more likely because it's not quite her thing.

After Bond rescues his woman and gets to destroy the end-of-the-world facility, almost capturing the bad guy but seeing him escape, I can't help but really like this movie. It's corny, but it's also got more of a heart than the other Bond movies. They tend to be all action and sexy ladies and gadgets and guns; this one has more slow moments and emotion. And there's not one gadget to be found.

I almost wake up Marvel during the wedding.

*Bond is getting married?*

The wedding is short but it's kinda wonderful. They're driving away and I wonder, when does Bond get a divorce? He's never married in the other films. But still, it's a nice moment.

There's the music again.

*We have all the time in the world, Marvel.*

That's the thing I believe.

I can be her secret agent and I can make sure I save her and I can stand with her as the sky falls, right? So that we end up driving off into the sunset and stopping the car to take the decorative flowers off and sharing a moment and—

*Watching my bride get shot in the head!*

My mouth is literally hanging open.

The bad guy is wearing a neck brace, but he's driving, and his bad woman accomplice has a machine gun that blasts Bond's car. He gets back in the car to give chase and . . .

*Seriously?*

Bond cradles his wife, and I glance down to see if Marvel is watching this. Thankfully she's still asleep. A policeman on a motorcycle shows up, and Bond holds his dead wife in his arms and kisses her. Then he gives the cop a calm and almost numb look.

"It's quite all right, really. She's having a rest. We'll be going on soon. There's no hurry, you see. We have all the time in the world."

Agent 007 kisses the wedding ring on her finger and then buries his face in her to weep. They show the bullet hole in the windshield of the car and the sad music plays and the credits come on. Bam, the end.

*Very unhappily ever after. Thanks for coming! Good night!*

The lights come back on, and I nudge Marvel from her nap. She's surprised how deep of a sleep she fell into.

"Did I miss anything?" she asks.

"Seriously, you haven't seen it?"

She yawns and wipes her eyes. "No, of course not. I don't like Bond movies."

She really and truly did this for me.

"In the end Bond saves the world and gets the girl."

"Don't they always end like that?"

*Not this time, Marvel.*

I take her hand and grip it firmly. Then I look up and notice the glowing chandelier in the center of the ceiling. There's a bluish sort of hue around it, and golden lines shoot out of it so that it resembles some kind of massive star above us. It shines down carefully on us while we leave.

*There's no hurry, you see.*

Yeah, right. Speak for yourself, Bond.

## 15

I don't want to take Marvel back to the house where she and her aunt are staying. Nor do I want to take her back to my house. I don't want to have coffee with her and I don't want to walk on the sidewalk. I want to find some little hidden farmhouse in the Alps just like Bond and Tracy and cuddle up to stay warm.

Instead, we sit on a bench in the theater lobby. We figure we'll be asked to leave soon enough, but for now Marvel is still waking up and I'm still trying to process the saddest 007 film I've ever seen.

"Wouldn't it be wonderful to go to the Alps someday?" I ask. "Do you know how to ski?"

"Never tried. Not sure if you know this, but Chicago doesn't have any hills."

"Funny. I've gone in upper Michigan. I'm not bad."

"I could be on the bunny slopes while you go up the mountain."

"Uh-uh," I say. "I'm staying behind with you."

"You're going to teach me to ski?"

"I'll help. Don't think I'm much of a teacher. But I can be there in case you need someone to fall into."

"Aww," Marvel says.

"So your perfect place—where would that be?"

She rubs her hands together as if she's cold, even though she has her long jacket and wool cap on. Her eyes flicker around as she contemplates the question.

"I don't know if there is a 'perfect place.' I like to think of having my lovely day."

"Your lovely day?"

"Yeah. The kind that feels perfect. I see water—calm, not moving. And I'm floating on it. Slowly. Just gliding through rose petals. Red and white and pink and yellow and orange and blue and peach. Like I'm floating on a rainbow."

Marvel is somewhere else now. She's in her lovely day, drifting away from this theater and from me. I lock my arm around hers.

"So what are you doing?" I ask. "Or where are you going?"

She shakes her head. Those eyes find mine, and I see absolutely no distance or hesitation in them. They're raw and real, a photo that's unaltered, no filter necessary.

"I'm not going anywhere. I'm just sitting and taking it in. There's no need to look over my shoulder. No need to worry about storms coming. No fear that the boat will start leaking or get overturned. There's this silent blanket around me and every color I can imagine."

"One thing's missing to make it perfect," I say.

Her face lights up. "Okay, fine. You can come along if you *have* to."

She leans over and gives me a peck on the cheek, then tells me we better get out of here before someone calls security.

This isn't a hidden barn in the Alps, and it's not the perfect day that Marvel dreams about. But it's still something.

# 16

A long red line streaks down the guy's chin while he runs in the dark. He wipes it, smearing it into a messy dark stain on the side of his face. I try to see who it is, but I can only see his back. Until he turns.

Then, even though it's almost pitch black, I see Seth Belcher's angry eyes looking back at me. They look full of tears. I try to call his name, but he keeps running.

I can't follow him, not in dreamworld here. But I can hear his footsteps fade away.

The next thing I see is the morning light sneaking into my room. For a moment I think about calling Seth. Just to tell him to be extra careful today. To be on the lookout for something, something I can't explain. But I know I'll sound like a tool, and Seth probably wouldn't listen to me anyway.

I decide to look for him at school.

It's strange how much can happen in a year. Last March I was wishing summer was already here. Not thinking I'd have to get a second job (because Barton hadn't crashed my car yet). Not having any idea I'd get a job at Fascination Street Records (because who knew people actually bought vinyl). Not knowing a girl like Marvella Garcia existed (not to mention would actually come into that very record store). Not expecting that one of our classmates would be found dead that same exact day (or my best friend would be found dead months later).

Lots of *nots* packed into place there. And now I was trying to find Seth Belcher, a kid I didn't even know a year ago, nor would have imagined I'd be friends with. Though the term *friends* is stretching it a bit.

When I find him I notice his Black Flag T-shirt. I assume they're some rock band. Some angry, rebellious rock band. I'll have to remember to Google them later.

I greet him the way I might have greeted Devon a year ago. But Seth barely even looks at me.

"Any high school drama lately?" I ask.

"Who wants to know?"

I laugh and then look at his face and realize he's not joking.

"Just asking. Curious. Haven't seen you around."

"Yeah, I know."

I can't tell if he "knows" because he's been avoiding me or because I've just neglected hanging out.

"So, anything exciting going on?"

He stops and looks at me with a literal sneer on his face. "Why are you so curious?"

Enough with this.

"What's wrong?" I demand.

"What?"

I shake my head. "Seriously, man. I don't get you."

"Then don't try to."

"I mean—I'm just asking—"

But Seth just walks away.

He was like this the first time I rescued him from getting beat up. And the second. I wasn't quite on time to save him from his Halloween altercation.

*You weren't on time to save Devon on Halloween either.*

I head to my next class feeling like there's more I should be doing. That I'm missing the boat here. I don't know.

Maybe I can invite him to church.

*Too corny.*

Maybe I can go back to that fight club thing with him.

*Too crazy.*

Maybe I can hold some kind of birthday bash for myself in a week and invite him.

*He won't come.*

In class, while the English teacher talks about a book I haven't been reading, I doze off and see Seth again. This time covered in blood. Running. And he turns to ask me why I'm not helping him. Why I'm not standing next to him and trying to help.

"Brandon?"

I look around and see the class staring at me.

"I'm sorry, did I interrupt your little nap?"

The teacher forces me to stop thinking of Seth and the blood and the dream. For now.

# 17

**You working?**

At first I assume it's a text from Marvel, but then I see it's coming from Frankie. He's not an avid texter, so I reply quickly.

**Yeah. Slow night.**

**I'll be there in five minutes**, Frankie writes.

If it were anybody else I'd text back asking what was going on. But knowing Frankie, I don't bother. He wouldn't respond anyway.

Soon the door to the record shop swings open and Frankie rushes in, out of breath. "Brandon, you've gotta come with me."

"I'm the only one here," I say.

"Then lock the doors and come back later."

"I can't—"

"It's your buddy Seth," Frankie says. "He's gonna be hurt tonight."

"What? What are you talking about?"

"Just come."

This time I don't hesitate. I follow him out of the record store and make sure the door is locked.

Once we're driving, Frankie tells me what's happening.

"They've been planning this for a while," he says as he whips around a corner and heads down Route 31.

"Planning what? Who're you talking about?"

He looks at me. "Who do you think?"

I didn't need to ask. I just thought all the stuff with Greg Packard was done with.

"How do you know?"

"Because I know," Frankie says.

"For how long? Were you ever going to tell me?"

"Don't defend him. My football season ended 'cause of that guy. Maybe even my career—"

"That's crazy. It was Greg's fault."

"Ever since Seth showed up, things have gotten out of hand. And yeah, I blame him."

"Do you blame me too?"

Frankie doesn't reply, which I take as a yes.

"So where are we going? And why are you taking me there?"

"I'm just—after Devon—after everything. After that stupid school assembly on bullying—I don't know."

"What's gonna happen, Frankie? Another strip-down? Tying him to another headstone?"

"No, it's not . . ." His voice trails off. He's got his phone out on his lap and glances at the GPS.

"Frankie, man, where are we going?"

"Some farm. Logan has an uncle or something who lives

on a big farm with horses and corn and all that. They're taking Seth there."

I wonder if this has anything to do with Devon's death. But that's crazy; it was Marvel's uncle who did that, not a bunch of football jocks. But I recall my dreams, and I can't help but think that Seth's gonna die tonight.

"What are they gonna do to him?" I ask.

"I don't know," Frankie says. "I didn't hear. All I managed to get was the address. There's a bunch of them going."

"To do *what*?" I yell.

"I told you, I don't know. That's why we're going there."

I feel helpless and angry. I feel my hand curl up in a fist as I clench my teeth and look out the dark window.

*Jeremy Simmons.*

Once again, I get a crazy thought about the scary guy Seth introduced me to—at a fight club, believe it or not. I think about trying to buy a gun from him. It could only lead to trouble, but right now I wish I had one just to do something to stop Greg and the rest of them. The very first time I helped Seth out, when he was being beaten up by Greg and Sergio, I was able to grab a bat and use it. Or at least try to look like I was using it.

"What are we gonna do when we get there?" I ask.

"I don't know," Frankie says. "But you're going to stay hidden in the car, got that? I'll get out and see what's happening, and if I need help—*if*—then you can help me."

"They're not going to listen to you."

"Maybe not," he says, checking his phone again for directions. "But maybe I can keep things from getting as bad as they could be."

"Yeah, that's pretty encouraging."

I picture Seth all bloody and terrified, sprinting in the dark and asking why I'm not helping him.

*I'm gonna help you, buddy, in whatever way I can.*

The farm is in the middle of nowhere. Way out in the country. The very *dark* country. I've always thought it's wild how dense the Chicago suburbs can be, but you drive about an hour further west and you have nothing. Just flat fields and farms.

We know we've arrived when we see a row of cars parked alongside a fenced-off field. There are lights on in a small house at the end of a very long driveway. A sense of dread fills me.

"Wait here, okay?" Frankie parks his car behind the last vehicle.

"For how long?"

He thinks for a minute. "Look, if I need you, I'll come get you."

"So why'd you bring me out here then?"

"Just in case," he says.

"In case what?"

"In case—in case things get out of hand."

I'm not sure what he means by that. I mean—here we are in the middle of the country in the dead of night and he's thinking things aren't already "out of hand"?

He shuts the door behind him, leaving me in silence.

I'm not very good at waiting. I check my phone, wondering if he might text. Maybe I should text Marvel to let her know what's happening. But I don't want her worried, so I don't.

Ten minutes and nothing. Then fifteen.

I can't keep still. And my phone's not communicating at all, so I'm restless.

Soon I've had enough. I get out into the cold night with a ceiling full of brighter-than-usual stars and head toward the farm.

By the time I reach the driveway and the edge of the fence, I can hear laughter. And screams. And something else.

Something really terrifying.

It's the sound of barking. Not just one dog, either.

*Uh-oh.*

Below the loud yelping are voices and hollering. I can't tell what's happening, but I jog alongside the fence toward the noise.

Then a flashlight—no, more of a spotlight—bursts over the field, and I actually dive to the ground.

I see a figure in some kind of weird outfit. Thick black pants and a heavy coat. He's the one screaming. Seth.

The voices are coming from over behind the fence. I see only outlines of figures standing near the spotlight on the pasture.

The voices are yelling and arguing while Seth is screaming and standing there in the middle of the field in this bulky clothing. His head keeps turning like he's expecting someone to appear.

The dogs aren't barking anymore.

Seth begins to run. Not that fast, since he's wearing something that appears heavy to move in.

A high-pitched voice yells out a command, but I can't make it out. *Find* maybe? Not *fetch*. Maybe *fight*.

Suddenly two German shepherds are racing over the field toward the shuffling Seth.

Unbelievable.

They're the two biggest dogs I've ever seen in my life. They're like small horses. Only faster and leaner. One is darker than the other, but both look mean and intent on getting their prey.

There's no way anybody could outrun those dogs. Even wearing shorts and track shoes. They tear into Seth's arms, and he sways and shakes and fights them off.

The chanting and applause begin. More yelling too. Seth is screaming and hollering and crying, and the crowd beyond, by the light, are mostly hooting and hollering.

This is sick.

I don't think. I climb through the wooden fence and then start sprinting toward the attacking dogs, screaming.

"Here I'm here come on here get me!" I'm yelling as loud as I can.

The cheering stops and the spotlight moves and I hear someone call out my name. I'm pretty sure it's Frankie, but the dogs notice me, and one decides I'm a little more meaty than Seth. Or maybe he knows I'm not wearing any kind of protective covering.

I start to run away from Seth now that I have one of the dogs after me.

"Cut cut cut cut cut cut cut cut!" the piercing voice cries out.

Both dogs stop and sit. Just like that. They're sitting and watching us now.

Frankie is still yelling out my name. Something else is

happening by the farmhouse and spotlight, but I don't care what might be occurring. I rush over to Seth and grab him and lead him away. The two dogs are sitting still, but I'm just waiting for another command. "Eat them for dinner" or something.

By the fence where I climbed through, I need to help Seth between the wooden boards. I don't dare take off this suit of his until we reach the car.

"Brandon," a voice behind us shouts out.

It's not Frankie this time.

"I see you, Brandon," he screams.

The guy is mocking me. And I'd bet all the money I have that it's Greg.

Seth sounds out of breath, his voice quavering, mumbling words I can't understand. He has spit dripping from his mouth, and his eyes are glassy and wet. I don't let him go until we reach Frankie's car. Then I look back, but no one is following us.

Seth is in a bit of a daze. I guess I can understand why.

His heavy coat and thick pants look like a snowsuit. I get the jacket off of him, then just open the car door and shove him in the backseat.

I'm so incensed that I start to run back to the driveway and the dogs and the voices and the idiots who did this to Seth.

*Remember last time you did something like that?*

The party. Yeah. I remember. It doesn't stop me. Frankie getting his arm busted and then Devon turning up missing. I'm halfway down the driveway, not worrying about any of that, when I see Frankie running toward me.

"We have to go."

"Why'd you let them do that?" I shout at him.

He almost plows into me, then turns me around and pulls me with him. "Now, Brandon."

"Give me a break. I want to—"

"He's got a gun," Frankie says.

I stare at him. "Who does?"

"The guy—the owner of the dogs. We need to leave."

"Who is it?"

Frankie looks scared. As if he's seen a ghost or something.

"I don't know, but he's just—he's not right. We gotta go."

"Is Greg—?"

"Yeah, but he's just drunk and being stupid."

"Who else—?"

Frankie's already on the street, close to his car, still pulling me along. The guy with the gun doesn't scare me. I want to show him he doesn't scare me.

I see Devon's face the night after he pulled a gun on Carlos. How scared he happened to look, yet at the same time a bit delirious in his bravery.

*Don't be like Devon.*

It was like an ad showing someone stupid and then saying, "Don't do this."

Yeah.

I follow Frankie and get in the backseat of his car with Seth. Frankie peels out and heads back the way we came. Driving a lot faster.

# 18

"I don't know what to say," I tell Seth.

He looks out of it. For a moment I wonder if he's on something—maybe some drug from his fight club buddy Jeremy. I look up at Frankie but don't get anything.

The farm. The field. The *dogs*.

*Two attacking German shepherds. Is this real?*

I look back at the dirt road we're still on but don't see anybody following us.

"How many were there?" I ask Frankie.

"I don't know. Ten or more. I got there right when they were putting the suit on him."

"Did they hurt you?" I ask Seth.

Nothing. He doesn't say a word.

I wipe sweat from my forehead and realize I'm still out of breath.

"Seth, man, are you okay?"

He just wipes his nose but looks ahead. I can't tell what

he's thinking or feeling, but I can't demand some kind of reaction from the guy.

"I tried to make them stop," Frankie says.

"What's with the guy who owns the farm?" I ask.

Frankie curses and says he doesn't know or want to know. "That guy. Man. He was like *The Silence of the Lambs*."

"Hannibal Lecter?"

"No. The other guy. The weirdo who's got the girl in the well. That one."

I have to think to remember it, and then I really wish I hadn't.

"Ugh" is all I can say.

"Yeah. Just—creepy. With the dogs. And he talked really strange. He was like speaking another language with the dogs."

"German?" I say, kinda trying to be funny but realizing no joke is funny right now.

"No. Some language I've never heard."

We get to the end of the dirt lane and then turn onto a regular paved road. I breathe a bit easier knowing we're leaving this place behind.

I hear Seth mumble and turn toward him. He's still facing the front and staring without really seeing anything.

"What'd you say?"

He just keeps talking.

"It would have been better had I remained as I was," Seth says. "To have this illusion—this brief taste of life—only to see it snatched away, to be condemned once more to eternal oblivion . . ."

Then he says something else under his breath.

"Seth—what are you talking about?"

I shake his arm, but he doesn't look at me. Frankie looks back at me with a disgusted look on his face.

There's a lot more I want to say to him, but for now we have to get this guy back home. Whatever planet Seth happens to be on doesn't concern us. But Greg—enough's enough. And I said that last Halloween.

*The bullying should've been over.*

I'm learning something about this life. Nothing is ever fully over. Carlos escapes and is still out there. My father is still missing. Devon's family still grieves. Marvel is still haunted by what God told her.

And I'm still here. Trying to end these not-so-happy stories. Trying.

Trying and failing.

# 19

We watch Seth walk to the front door of his house and head inside. I wonder for a moment if his parents keep the door unlocked all the time or only when he's out.

"He's always so grateful," Frankie says.

"I think he's embarrassed."

Frankie shakes his head. "No. He's angry. He tried fighting back, but there were too many of them. He was punching and screaming when they were putting him in that suit."

As we pull out of the driveway, I look at the coat and pants of the protective suit.

"Did you see if he got bit up at all?" I ask Frankie.

"I could see blood on his arms."

I clench my fists. "What were they thinking?"

"Greg's like one of those guys who beats animals. You

know? You hear about them on the news or the Internet and you go 'What a sick freak,' but you're also fascinated."

"There's nothing fascinating about his hatred."

"They were all drunk and maybe high," Frankie adds.

"I don't care if they invented a new kind of drug. I'm telling the cops."

"Didn't we go down this road before?"

He drives for a moment and then I put my hand on his arm, telling him to pull over. Not asking, but telling him. I want him to look at me. He slows down and then slides the car onto the side of the road. I can't help but let out a curse as I look at my buddy.

"I recall that I went down this road," I say. "You didn't because you were ticked about your arm being broken. I get it. I've said it before, but I'll say it again: *I'm sorry.* But I was just trying to help a kid out and I can't—"

"Why do you care so much about this guy?" Frankie asks.

There's anger in his normally bright and cheerful eyes.

"Maybe because nobody else does."

"Don't you have enough to deal with without trying to help Seth out?"

I shake my head. "You called me tonight, right? *You* did. So why are you laying into me?"

"I was worried for the guy's life."

"And so am I. I just want it to stop."

"Going to the cops?" Frankie says. "You think that'll do any good?"

"I don't know."

"They really helped with Devon. Oh, wait. No, they didn't. How about with Greg and Seth? Let's see. Nope."

A car passes us and slows down to see what we're doing stopped on the side of the road. I wave just to be annoying.

"Let it die down," Frankie says.

"Look—I was the one who came up with the idea of messing with Greg's car. I feel partially responsible."

"Greg knows that."

"Yeah, but he doesn't care," I say.

Frankie gazes into the front windshield. I know him well enough to know he's done talking about this.

"You can keep driving. Just drop me back off at the record store."

We end things in a very nonchalant see-you-tomorrow way. I go back into the store and start closing down things like I would do any other night.

Before leaving, I hear the blurp of a text message echo in the store. I head over to the counter where I left my phone, figuring it might be Frankie with some final thought. Instead I see Seth's name.

**Sorry for not thanking you guys. Sometimes I don't say anything because I'm just trying to figure out the right words to say what I'm feeling. I'm still figuring that out, but I'm grateful you helped out. Please don't do anything else. Like going to the cops or school or parents. Okay? Please promise me you won't.**

I look up from the phone and stare at a poster on the wall for a film about The Doors called *When You're Strange*. Then I read the text again and reply.

**Okay. No problem. Did you get any bad bites?**

I wait for a few minutes to see if he replies, but I get nothing. I sigh and then head home. I hear The Doors song that my coworker and resident hippie Phil loves to blast.

**GLORY**

*"When you're strange, faces come out of the rain."*

Back outside in the cold, I look around to see any faces. Friend or foe. The list of people I need to keep an eye out for is starting to lengthen. But thankfully, there's no one around. At least no one that I can see.

# 20

I'm eighteen today.

I don't feel old or young or even different. But the morning of March 18 reminds me that life in the last year has become very different, and thinking about all of that stuff makes me feel very old. A drunk of a father abandoning his family because of fear of jail time for abusing his kids. A best friend dead because of some murderer or *murderers* in our town. The uncle of the girl I love just so happening to be that killer. And then there's Marvel.

Yes, there's Marvel.

I check my phone and see that she's already sent me a morning text. This makes me smile. A very young-feeling smile.

**Happy birthday, Brandon!**

**We have a fun day ahead of us. So glad for the sun even if it's cold.**

**I'm glad God allowed me to find Fascination Street Records and thankful I discovered the singer called Brandon Jeffrey. It's been fun collecting his albums.** ☺

**Will see you soon, but here's a nice little blog post since you're probably the only person who reads them.**

I can't keep a grin off my face as I text her back. **You are awesome, you know that?**

**Yes**, she replies.

**Thank you!** I type.

Marvel and her blogs. Speaking of fascination . . . *fascinating* is exactly what they are. They've been like this window into her heart and soul. Sometimes I don't fully understand what her words mean, but that's what I like about them. Sometimes—no, many times—I imagine she's talking about me.

And today, I'm pretty positive that's the case.

**18**

Serenade me to sleep

And see me awaken on your lawn

With songs that sound like the sun and have its morning splendor

The sketches in the clouds all start to look a little like you

I run through puddles and realize they're mirages on the sidewalks

I feel sweat and see the subzero temperatures

Some things aren't fair but some things aren't like you

I wake up to a star-filled bout of wonder in my soul

I watch from afar and see you adrift

Floating so high it frightens my soul a bit

But you descend close enough for me to see your smile

And it all feels better

It doesn't belong to me nor does it rest at my bedside

But it parasails on the horizon and I know it's out there somewhere

The simple sweet solitary smile

I can rest my head in it

Memorizing it for my dreams

Raising it up like a glass to toast in the sky

Treasuring it on dark dreary days promised to me

Eighteen years and yet I've only found a love like this once

Ten months given to me

Yet even the moon can promise the sun tomorrow

I can simply promise today

Happy days handed to me time and time again

I won't let go as long as I can

    I'm sitting on the edge of my bed, still for a moment, surprised again. There is a surge inside that vows one more time with every single fiber of my being the following:
*I won't let you go either, Marvel.*
*There will be many more months and years.*
*I'm promising tomorrow if it's the last thing I do.*
    I hear my mother calling me for breakfast. Ah, the

turning-eighteen honorary breakfast. That's why I'm smelling bacon.

As I head downstairs, I have another thought.

*I don't want you on my lawn or floating on the horizon or leaving once your sun rises.*

No.

I want Marvel there when I wake up. The very *moment* I wake up. And the moment I fall asleep.

It's not too much to want or ask for. It's my birthday. Maybe, just maybe . . .

# 21

Marvel wears a red sweater/skirt combo. I don't know if it's new or some retro piece—but this is Marvel, so I can guess. The skirt hovers over her knees and she wears a plaid scarf around her neck and a plaid shirt tied around her waist. This is complemented by ankle-high boots with buckles.

"I've never paid as much attention to someone's outfits as I do to yours," I tell her after she greets me with a hug and a kiss on the cheek.

"Good to hear," she says. "You *should* pay attention. It's hard work to be this fashionable at this price."

"Thank you for your blog," I tell her.

"Thank you for being born."

"Not sure I had much to do with that."

We walk down the hallway that might as well be empty as far as we're concerned.

"True, but at least you've made some good choices in your eighteen years."

"How so?" I ask.

"How you are. The way you act. The things you think. The way you always smile at me."

"I can't help it."

"But you can—that's the beauty of it. Things are second nature to you. Like your kind heart."

I don't consider my heart as particularly "kind," but I'm not going to argue.

"I think you're being extra nice to me 'cause it's my birthday," I tell her.

"Of course I am."

"Will this keep up? All day?"

She brushes back her dark locks and smiles. "Of course."

"And all night?"

The smile doesn't fade, but she tightens her lips and doesn't say a word. Then she points her head to class and waves bye to me.

I can't help thinking of the classic line from *Dumb & Dumber*.

*"So you're telling me there's a chance."*

Yes, possibly, there might be a chance. And if allowed, I'd take it. In a heartbeat. Without hesitation. Without any further thought.

It's probably a good thing that girls are smarter than boys.

The day is not much different, other than the happy birthday well-wishes from my friends and even some teachers. But near the end of the day, as I'm counting the seconds when I'll be heading out to hang out with Marvel and do something-and-anything, Seth comes up to me.

"Hey, Brandon. Got you a present."

He hands me a black CD in a plastic holder.

"I burned some of my favorite songs. Listen to it 'cause it tells a pretty cool story."

I hold up the disc. "Cool. Thanks."

He looks nervous for some reason. Maybe because he's doing something nice and it feels a little unusual for him.

"Well, have a good one," he says and quickly disappears.

When I get to my locker, I toss the CD into my backpack and figure I'll listen to it later. *After* hanging out with Marvel. I'm not assuming there's any kind of sweet, romantic music on this.

*Definitely nothing sweet.*

Marvel and I get inside my Honda and I start the car, wondering where we're going. She answers by leaning over and kissing me, a kiss that literally takes my breath away since it lasts so long and I can't swim to the surface for air. Not that I mind drowning like this. I feel her hand against my cheek, gently pulling me toward her.

"Wow" is all I can say when I finally am able to talk and breathe and think.

Marvel gives this look as if she knows. Not a cocky look, but rather the confident kind any female might give to a guy like me. Knowing that I'm sorta helpless, like a puppy wagging its tail, wanting a treat.

"So are you going to drive?" she asks.

"I don't have to," I say. "We can stay right here."

Marvel knows this particular look of mine. "No, I think you do, Mr. Jeffrey. Let's hang out awhile. Then find somewhere where I can buy you dinner."

"A steak house?" I joke.

"I didn't know Chick-fil-A served steak," she jokes back.

"You don't have to buy me anything."

"I know. So drive."

"But where? You tell me."

She shakes her head, and I admire the red beanie that matches the rest of her ensemble perfectly. *Ensemble* is a word Marvel likes to use, so now I do too.

"Go wherever you'd like to hang out with me for a while," she says. "Then it will be up to me where we go next."

So I do. The destination is no surprise to her, of course. It's just the first thing that pops to my mind. A safe place. A place that feels a bit like home, more so than the house where my mother and brothers live with me.

When we park and get out of the car, she smiles. "Did you forget to tell me you had to work tonight?"

We walk across the street to the record store.

"Well, actually, yeah, but the good news is that you'll be getting a check for it next week."

"Please never stop those checks from coming," Marvel says.

"As long as you're nearby I won't. I promise."

# 22

"Do you believe we take the memories with us?"

The question comes out of nowhere. Like so many of Marvel's questions. I'm not sure exactly what she means, and I think she knows that clueless look of mine by now.

"When we die," she continues. "Do you think we'll remember what happened down here?"

I shrug. "Yeah, probably."

She laughs, and her eyes look like they belong to a pretty little girl who has just been handed a colorful balloon. We've left the record store and are standing on the sidewalk next to my car, and I'm waiting for her to tell me where to go.

"You know how many times I've said something and you've just shrugged?"

I almost do that exact thing again, then stop myself. We both laugh.

"Seriously," Marvel says. "Think about it."

"Well, I guess—"

She puts a finger over my lips. "I said *think* about it. For maybe longer than a second or two."

So I do. I look at her, then at the hood of my Honda, then back at her. I think of heaven, and I can't imagine that God won't let us remember our lives on earth.

"I think we'll take them with us," I say. "At least the good memories."

Marvel keeps that grin on her face. "That's what I was hoping you'd say. I think that too. And I'm counting on it."

Before I can say anything else, she starts walking down the sidewalk. "Come on."

So I follow her like I've been doing ever since she arrived in my life.

"Where are we going?" I ask.

"To find your birthday present," she calls out, starting to run.

I can only smile and shake my head and try to keep up with her. It's always an impossibility. I think I knew that from the very start.

Through the doors and the hallways and the rows of books, we walk holding hands and laughing and whispering and occasionally taking a photo. Marvel tells me she chose the library because it's open and it's big and it's full of a billion different words we wish could be spoken between us. Then we split up to pick out a book for each other that the other *has* to read.

In the large atrium at the entrance, we sit on a bench and show our "gifts" to each other. She goes first, handing me a hardcover book.

"*Pride and Prejudice*?" I read.

"It's not a question," Marvel says with a giggle. "I'm betting you haven't read this."

"Maybe in English class. I'm not sure."

"It's such a great love story. Elizabeth and Darcy are so well matched. They're honest with each other—eventually—and you just know these two will be happy together. I read it when I was in junior high and have loved it ever since."

"It might take me till graduation to read this," I tell her.

"That's only a few months away."

"I was talking about college graduation."

She laughs and nudges me with her arm. "Okay, now let me see what you got." She tries to peek around my side where I'm concealing the book.

"I think I want to check a different book out."

"Stop it. Come on, show me."

"I think I didn't understand the assignment," I tell her.

I was just going for laughs, but after hearing about the meaningful book she picked out for me, I feel like a bit of a tool. Or maybe just a boy.

"No changing your mind," Marvel says, trying to reach around me.

We ignore the people looking our way as we wrestle with each other in the lobby of the library. She finally manages to pull the book away from me and reads the title out loud.

"*Panda's Day Off.*"

She gives me an exaggerated strange look.

"Look, it's award-winning. It's got that seal. It won the Calcutta medal."

Marvel keeps laughing at me. "It's Caldecott. It looks deep. Very, very deep."

"No, now wait. I know it's just a kids' book. But the message is very meaningful."

"And I take it you had time to read it moments ago, right?"

I laugh. "Well, yeah. Took about two minutes."

"Such deep thoughts."

"No, but listen. The book is all about the panda deciding to take a day off and explore life and have fun away from the kid he belongs to. And he has the most amazing day of his life. This is all symbolic."

"Symbolic of what?" she asks, surely knowing where I'm going.

"Symbolic of *you*. You're my day off, Marvel. You've always been my day off. From my life. From all of it. Every moment with you has always been the best day of my life."

Her playful glance turns serious, and I see tears appear in her eyes.

"I didn't mean to get all mushy," I say, feeling bad.

"Suddenly this might be the best book I've read in my life," Marvel says, reaching over and kissing me.

There are more memories, some simple blinks, others floating bubbles. Walking down the sidewalk. Heading into Walgreens. Going for sandwiches at the coffee shop. Driving around listening to music. All the while sometimes talking and sometimes allowing the silence to cover us. We take pictures to document the occasion, but I know they're unnecessary. I wouldn't forget this time even if someone erased every single memory from my mind. I think some memories get stored in your heart, and when your brain has finally gone and you don't have any cells left to run it, those memories are all you have left. They pass with you to eternity.

As ten o'clock approaches, Marvel tells me to drive to the riverwalk. We get out and walk toward the edge of the water, the wind leaving us alone and the temperature not too cold for a March night. I follow her to the place where we stood not long ago and I came up with the idea for Marvel to marry me. I guess I actually did propose to her, even though she didn't take me seriously. I've thought about it a lot since that night.

I still think it's a glorious idea.

"Come here," she says.

"What?"

"Walk with me."

"Where are we going?"

"Do we have to be going somewhere? I just want to hold your hand and walk. And to do it as if we've done it a thousand times before. To do it like it's only two legs walking instead of four. To hold hands like it's as natural as walking itself."

I grasp her hand and look at her with a laugh. "That's a lot of pressure for holding hands."

"No pressure. Not with me. You know that."

And I do. We hold hands and walk as though we've been walking hand in hand for the last ten years.

I wonder if my heart can feel this full for ten years or twenty or fifty. I don't know, but the way I feel, it sure seems like it.

Marvel guides me to a gazebo stretching out over the inlet

of water off the Fox River. The structure isn't lit, but the glow of the moon brightens it enough for me to be able to see her expression of joy.

"Don't tell me you want to go swimming," I say.

"Would you if I wanted to?"

"Yes. But only if you jumped in first."

She laughs and takes something out of her coat pocket. I see two round objects attached by a wire.

"What is that?" I ask.

She doesn't answer but takes out her phone and sets it on the rail of the gazebo, and I realize that the "balls" are speakers. She plugs the wire into her iPhone and a song begins to play. A slow one, just a piano.

I'm not sure where the song came from or who performed it or anything about it, but I don't care. I just watch as Marvel closes her eyes and slowly starts to circle her head in motion to the music. Then the rest of her body follows, with her hands swaying and her legs shifting.

That smile never leaves her lips.

There's a sadness at the start of this piano piece, but then it starts to build and grow brighter. I stand at the entrance to the gazebo just watching—her silhouette against the glow of the moon on the water—her figure twirling away and moving back and forth—and suddenly I feel a little lost. In a good way. Like you might feel when you're running away from something and finally find yourself in some strange but safe place, out of breath with muscles burning. The music fades and it feels like everything around us does as well, except for Marvel and that glow behind her.

"Are you going to let me dance all alone?" she calls out.

"I like watching you."

"And I like dancing."

I realize something I forgot. "I didn't take your picture."

"Yes, you did," she says. "That high-powered Canon inside your head."

She laughs and then seems to float over to me. Another slow-moving song starts to play on the tiny speakers, this one with a female singer who sounds like an angel. Marvel wraps her arms around my waist and rests her head against my shoulder. I fit around her and close my eyes and imagine our embrace never ending.

"So is this my birthday present?" I ask.

"Yes," she says, her voice soft and relaxed.

"Can I ask for a few more presents?"

"You can ask," she says, moving and looking up at me with that knowing smile. "Hey—listen to the next song."

It's slow and sad, which seems to be the theme tonight, but the singer has a youthful voice, high-pitched. Except . . .

"It's Spanish."

"Really?" Marvel jokes.

"What is she singing about?" I ask.

"Maybe you should learn the language."

"Well, I guess I need to imagine then."

In another place and time, this song would be ours. Maybe the one we'd dance to on our wedding day. I'd know every word and I'd be able to speak them to her. We wouldn't be shadows undercover but would be lit up under the spotlight. I wouldn't have to wonder and want to be with Marvel, to take her in my arms and do everything I've ever imagined doing with her without hesitation or fear.

Another place and time . . .
I have this realization, this belief.
*It doesn't have to be another one. It can be now.*
Then I have another. I realize that slow-dancing with this girl in this unseen spot like I'm doing right now might be the best birthday present I'll ever receive. And I'm grateful.

# 23

It's easy to forget all the bad things swirling around outside. My birthday and all the things Marvel said and did not only help me forget, they allow me to forge ahead with life. Of course, my dream of spending the night with her doesn't happen. I never asked because the day had been pretty amazing. I didn't want to ruin it.

The next couple of days are surprisingly uneventful and normal. That changes when I see Jeremy Simmons open the door to the record store Thursday night.

Harry is sitting behind the counter and greets Jeremy as he walks by. I'm in the back of the store going through a box of T-shirts that just came in, and I don't hear him reply. His narrow eyes focus on me and don't show any kind of emotion. The serpent tattoo seems to crawl over his neck.

"Brandon," he says like a drill sergeant calling attention.

"Yeah."

Harry's watching, and I know that he'll come to my side if this guy starts punching me.

"Where's Seth?"

I don't answer him right away. My brain is too slow and the rest of me is too scared.

"Where is he?" he repeats.

"I don't know," I say.

I haven't talked to Seth, or even seen him, since he gave me the CD—which I still haven't listened to.

"He owes me money."

Jeremy is talking loud enough for Harry to hear, prompting him to walk over toward us.

"I saw him a couple of days ago," I offer.

"You don't know if he split?" Jeremy asks.

I'm not sure if he's on something but he walks and looks wired, like a fuse that's lit and burning.

"Can I help you?" Harry asks.

"Don't think so, Curly."

Harry doesn't smile; he just looks at me. "Everything okay?"

I nod. "Yeah."

"Your buddy owes me some major cash," Jeremy says.

I'm tempted to reply that Jeremy is as much of a "buddy" to Seth as I am, but I'm not going to say anything that could get him more irritated.

"I don't know where he is. I can try texting him or something."

Jeremy studies me for a second. His thick mustache droops over his mouth and seems so out of place with the rest of him.

"I just want to make sure he's not doing something really stupid," he says.

Harry is still standing there overseeing the situation. Jeremy ignores him.

"Do you want me to text him?" I ask.

"You tell him he better pay up in the next week or I'm coming to get what's mine. Tell him I'll find him too. Doesn't matter if he's decided to go cross-country for some reason."

It doesn't sound like anything Seth would do.

"I don't think he's going to do that."

Jeremy only laughs and shakes his head. "You text him and tell him I stopped by. You got it?"

I nod.

Jeremy shifts his head toward Harry. "This place make any money?"

"We make it work," Harry says in the most unfriendly voice I've ever heard him use toward a customer. Though I don't really consider Jeremy to be shopping.

Jeremy flashes teeth that are chipped in a couple of places. "You're in the wrong business, buddy."

"And I think you're in the wrong store, *buddy*," Harry tells him.

Jeremy gives him a look that says, *I could take you down in two seconds*. And while it's probably true, I think it's awesome that Harry doesn't back down one bit.

"I'll be seeing you around, Brandon."

Muscles-and-mustache man walks out. Harry watches the door close and then turns toward me, shaking his head.

"What was that all about?"

"I don't know," I say. "Honestly."

"How do you know that guy?"

"My friend Seth—you know, the nerdy kid, he's been in here a few times—he introduced me."

"He looks like he needs a hug."

I laugh. "Yeah, I think he does."

"So what's up with Seth?"

"What do you mean?" I ask him.

"Why's he hanging around with that guy?"

I wonder whether to tell him the truth. I know I can trust Harry. He's not going to judge or give me a hard time about anything—not that he has a reason to do either in this case.

"I think—I don't *know*—but I think Seth buys drugs from him. Jeremy smokes pot, but he might sell too."

I don't bother mentioning the whole fight club thing. That's just plain weird.

"I'd stay away from him, Brandon. You have enough bad people in your life."

"I'm trying to," I say.

"And Seth—be careful with him too. Somebody like that—you don't want him sucking you into his mess."

I nod. I can't be around at all times to keep Seth from being bullied or hanging around with the wrong kind of people. Maybe one is the reason for the other, who knows. But I agree with Harry. There are too many messy people in my life already. The last thing I need is Jeremy coming by again.

The next time he might not be as cheery.

# 24

When I get home from work, I text Seth to tell him about Jeremy coming in. I'm not expecting a reply, but he answers me right away.

**What'd he say?**

**He said you owe him money and you better pay and you better not be driving across the country or something dumb like that. Where are you?**

There's a pause, but he finally writes, **I'm going to pay him.**

**What do you owe him for?**

Seth doesn't answer. I can understand.

**So where are you?** I write.

**I'm gone.**

**Gone where?**

**Just gone. No big deal.**

**Like out of town? Out of the country? In prison? On a date?**

I'm trying to be funny, but I'm betting Seth isn't amused.

**Did he say anything else?** Seth asks.

**Just that he'll find you.**

**Okay. Tell him I'll get him his money.**

I can't help but laugh. **Sure, hold on a minute, he's right here. ??!! YOU TELL HIM. I don't want to see him again.**

**In case he shows up.**

I type in my text quickly. **PAY HIM so he DOESN'T show up.**

**I will.**

**Everything okay?**

I can't help but ask. I've come to like Seth, for some reason. Maybe just because of how hard I've tried to keep him from getting his face smashed in. But there's something dorky yet defiant with this guy. From the comics he's always reading to his various Bruce Lee–inspired outfits.

I can see that he's typing a message, so I wait with the phone in my hand and the screen glowing.

**Wish there was something real. Wish there was something true.**

A very Seth-like statement.

**Some things are real & true**, I write.

**Gotta go.**

And that's that.

I decide to watch television with my brothers and text Marvel. I don't want to think about Jeremy and Seth anymore. Seth is probably building a rocket launcher in the woods somewhere. And it'll probably work too.

# 25

"So you hanging in there?"

Mom's question comes totally out of nowhere as she drives us home from Target. I realize it might look a little weird that I'm eighteen years old and still going to a department store to let my mother buy me some jeans and a few shirts, but I'm saving my money for other things and she offered. Probably because driving in the car together is the only time we have anything like a conversation.

It's not like we ever sit down and tell each other our thoughts and feelings. Sometimes I wonder what it'd be like to have sisters. Maybe Mom would have liked three girls instead.

"Yeah," I tell her, not really sure how I should be hanging in there.

"With your father being gone and all?"

I just shrug. "I don't have to worry about being punched in the face."

It's strange how truth really can set you free. I used to hide the abuse from my mother, carrying it around like a coiled but unbending water hose in the middle of winter. Now I can actually joke about my father hitting me, because Mom knows.

She grows silent, and tears form in her eyes.

*Good one, Brandon. Way to make Mom cry, you idiot.*

"I'm sorry. I was just kidding."

"I still wish you had told me," Mom says as she glances at me with sympathetic eyes. "You can tell me anything."

"I know that. Now."

"Do you worry much?" she asks.

"About what?"

"About your father showing up. About something else happening?"

"I think I worry more for Marvel and her psychopath of an uncle."

Mom nods. "I worry about that too. For both of you."

"I'm fine. He better not come looking for me."

Mom gives me one of those motherly protective what-am-I-going-to-do-with-you? looks.

"What?" I ask.

"You know—you are a lot like your father."

I hate hearing this even if it's true. "Yeah, and by the way, can we stop at the liquor store on the way home—I need some vodka."

"Brandon, stop that."

"Just sayin' . . ."

"Don't be disrespectful. It's not funny. I say that—about you being like your father—because he used to be so fearless. Taking on the world. Never backing down."

I look at Mom and shake my head. "Doesn't sound like Dad."

"That's who he used to be, until life chipped away at that courage. The courage that was accompanied with a lot of pride. But do you know something? You know what scared him more than anything else?"

*Running out of beer during a Bears game?*

I decide not to be funny, so I shake my head again.

"Becoming a father. When it came to being a dad, he just simply didn't know what to do. He believed he was a failure from the very beginning. And since you were his first, he felt like he was the biggest failure with you."

I glance at the stores on Randall Road and all the cars passing us by. I'm not sure what to say.

"It got easier with each son," Mom tells me. "At least that's what he believed."

"It helps to have the youngest be Carter. Mr. Nike himself."

"Yes, you're right."

She pauses and I look over at her, noticing lines that seem chiseled out under her eyes. Her skin looks pale and tough, like something that's been outside for too long in the cold Chicago winter.

"It's a terrible thing to have to look your children in the eyes when you feel like a failure," she says.

For a moment we're the only two people on this road. For the first time I see her as someone my age, someone anxious and curious and *young*. Worried and wondering about life and love and the rest of her future.

"You're not a failure," I tell her.

I don't look away, so when she glances back at me, I can see tired relief.

"You, Brandon . . . you're a blessing. Don't ever forget that. Okay?"

"I won't. And I'll try to remind Alex and Carter of that every day."

We both laugh. It's good to laugh. The world can't ever get enough of it.

# 26

Not long ago—sometimes it feels like just a blink—Marvel and I stood in Grant Park on a perfect afternoon. The wind purred against us, a sweet little whisper from Lake Michigan. This was the scene, seeing the slightly overcast sky begin to break while listening to the melancholy mood music from Alt-J, when I reached out. When I held Marvel for the first time. When the two of us became one for a nice little moment. Well, as close to one as she would allow us to be.

I think about that snapshot in time often. On this Saturday I wake up thinking of it again. There was no turning back after that moment at Lollapalooza. A sudden realization that this was more and it was real and somehow this girl liked me. For some reason I meant a lot to Marvel.

And I still do.

Today is her birthday. Mine feels like it was just yesterday. I didn't write a blog post or a poem or anything since I'm not a good writer. But I do have big plans for today and even bigger plans for tonight.

I actually feel my heart racing. I'm that excited, that anxious. I hear that sports saying in my head.

*Go big or go home.*

Not that I need that bit of encouragement. There's no way I'm not going to go big. No way I'm going to go home.

I call Marvel a little after eight.

"You awake?" I ask her.

"No, I'm sleep-talking."

"You must be dreaming."

"Yes. That's what I'm doing."

"Dreaming of the perfect guy wishing you a perfectly happy birthday."

"Oh, really?" Marvel says. "Well, then I better hang up and wait for that call."

I make a wounded sound.

"You know I'm kidding," she says.

"Yes, I do. Happy birthday, Marvel."

"Thank you."

"Any big plans for today?"

I hear her tired laugh. I imagine hearing it right next to me on a Saturday morning. Under covers and hidden by pillows that I have to dig out in order to see her face.

"Oh, I don't know," Marvel says. "I keep hearing about these grand plans and everything."

"They haven't changed."

"Does it involve a helicopter ride and a dinner date in an exotic city and then waiting to get a rose while I'm surrounded by twenty other ladies?"

"Oh, man," I say. "How did you know? Come on, that's not fair to guess the secret."

"I'm saying no to *The Bachelor*."

"Look, I'm just trying to find love," I joke.

"And here I thought you'd already found it."

I don't want to play around anymore. "I did find it. In a record store last summer."

"God works in mysterious ways, right?"

I glance out my window at the clouds in the bright sky. I nod and tell her, "Yes, he does."

"So when do I get to see you?" she asks.

"Not until later this afternoon."

"That late?"

"I have some things to do."

"Ah." She has a delightful sort of intrigue in her voice. "You still need to decorate the Marvel birthday float, right?"

"Yes. And get the fireworks ready."

"Very good."

"Are you still having lunch with your aunt?"

"Yes. And maybe with the cops too."

"They're still around?"

"Every now and then," she says. "They showed up last night. We told them it's my birthday today. Who knows? Carlos might actually remember and decide to do something dumb."

Maybe I should end up seeing her sooner rather than later.

"Brandon?"

"Yeah?"

"Don't go there," she says, reading my mind.

"What?"

"I know what you're thinking. I'm fine. Okay?"

"I know."

"Let's try to keep the world outside today."

"Yeah," I say. "I know. I'll try. I'll feel fine when you're by my side."

"My Superman," she says with a laugh.

"Yep, though you really don't want to see me in that tight suit. I like Batman better."

"You don't brood enough to be Batman. No, you're Superman." Her warm voice sounds like it's whispering in my ear.

"So you like DC Comics over Marvel?"

"Oh no," she says.

"What?"

"You're starting to sound like Seth."

I realize she's right. "Yeah, well, anything to try to relate to the guy. You know?"

"That's what makes you Superman."

"Look—I don't have any sort of blog to show you this morning."

"That's okay. That's my thing. I don't want you copying me."

I stand and grab the sheet of paper on my desk. "I do have a fun little thing I want to do with you today."

"Uh-oh. Do I have to work at the record store today?"

"No, no. But it does involve music. I know you love music."

"I love a lot of things."

"Of course you do. So here's the deal."

"Ooh, a deal?" she interrupts. "Do I need a Groupon to use it?"

I shake my head and laugh. "I think eighteen is looking a little feisty on you."

"Maybe it is. A new Marvel."

"Good. So I have a list of songs I want to share with you. My Marvel Birthday Playlist."

"Are there eighteen songs?"

"No. That'd be too cliché. No, I'm imagining that we've been together over the decades and I had to pick one song from each decade to sum up you and me and the two of us."

There's a pause, prompting me to ask if she's there.

"Yes, I'm here. So you're imagining we're vampires, huh? Part of the Twilight series?"

"No vampires," I say. "Just—we have a time machine. Let's say that."

"I like that."

"Every hour before I pick you up, I'll share one song. Okay? I'll tell you the first one now and then I'll text you the rest. So I'm not bugging you too much."

"You're not bugging me," she says in a serious tone. "This is such a sweet idea."

"Well, let's see what you think of the songs. I started in the 1940s."

"The forties? Oh, but the thirties were a much better decade."

I laugh. "You really did wake up on the witty side of the bed."

"Giddy," Marvel says. "That's how I feel."

"Good. Keep that feeling all day."

"I'll try."

"The song—well, all of these actually—was popular. It's 'Le Vie en Rose' by a woman named Edith Piaf."

My cell phone fills up with her laughter.

"What?" I ask.

"It's not 'Ee-dith.' It's pronounced 'Ee-dee.'"

"Oh, hush and listen to the song."

"It's French."

"Yes," I say. "Maybe you can find some way to translate it."

"I will talk to Mr. Google."

"More to come, okay, Miss Garcia?"

There's a pause before I go. "Brandon?"

"Yeah."

"Thank you."

"For the song?"

"Yes. For every song you've ever shared with me."

"I don't think there have been that many," I say.

"There's been one a day. And they're all glorious."

# 27

There's a weird feeling when you stand beside this kind of door, ready to unlock it and open it and step through. I feel like it's a gateway to possibility. That maybe somehow it can change lives. Maybe the fact that we're both eighteen and technically adults does mean something. Graduation is so close. *So* close. I want to take that time machine I told Marvel about and get to the day after. To know she's still beside me.

I pray daily for that to happen.

I have a second list that I made after the songs from the decades. It's a to-do list, something I rarely make, for the day. There are about twenty things on it: Going to a certain store. Checking in with another one. The florist, of course. The location and the setup for the evening.

There's also a person I need to talk to.

So hour by hour, I manage to cross the items off.

And all the while, I text Marvel my songs. They are tunes I wish I could have composed for her. Lyrics I wish I could have imagined. They're like a playlist of my soul. Music to listen to while standing beside this door.

Maybe Marvel is right. Maybe every day we do share a song with someone, whether it's one someone else created or one we wrote ourselves. I just know that I won't be literally singing them. The world doesn't need to hear that awful sound.

To follow my French forties song I picked a slow and sappy ballad. It's Elvis and maybe that's a corny and cliché thing, but the song is great. "Love Me Tender." It's perfect especially since it says "I'll be yours through all the years."

**I love that song,** Marvel replies.

**Thought you might.**

An hour later, I text her another one.

**For my sixties song that captures you/me/us, I chose "God Only Knows" by the Beach Boys.**

**Awwww,** she writes back. **Well, you know that they're right. Only God knows.**

One of the reasons I chose it. The song sounds like Marvel, the way she walks and the way everything in me pulses to those steps. It's the sound a smile would make if it could.

I have a bit of a delay on the seventies song because—well, it's happening. Things are taking a little longer than I expected, and I get a text from Marvel wondering when the next song is coming.

**Sorry! Yes. It's "Leather and Lace" by your gal Stevie Nicks.**

**That's quite some title.** ☺

**Have you heard it?** I ask.

**Yes. But need to check out the lyrics and read them more carefully.**

**Please do.**

Technically, this Stevie Nicks song is from 1981, but I don't think Marvel is going to proofread my playlist. It sounds like one of the Fleetwood Mac songs from the 70s.

The eighties come in the early afternoon as I begin to get truly impatient for tonight. I chose a song with a nod to Harry and the store and our experience at Lollapalooza.

**The Cure!** Marvel writes back. **My fave by them.**

I know that "Lovesong" is a big hit, just like all these others, but I'm not trying to be ultra-smart, going all Harry or Phil by picking obscure but brilliant tracks. I'm just going with classics. Ones I know.

Like "Wonderwall" by Oasis.

**So I'm your wonderwall?** Marvel writes to me.

Yes.

**What exactly IS a wonderwall?**

I have no idea. But you are one. This wonderful wall that keeps out the bad things.

**I like that,** she says. **But I thought you were going to be the one to save me, not vice versa.**

She has a point. **Salvation can come in lots of different forms.**

For the 00s or the aughts, I have us "Chasing Cars" with Snow Patrol.

**Perfect,** she writes me. **I think you've been sneaking into my bedroom and seeing my favorite songs.**

I'm paying off the cops.

**Can we forget the world tonight?**

Yes, I say.

And finally, the last song I send to her is one I text half an hour before picking her up.

"XO" by Beyonce

She writes back right away. **Such a fun & sweet playlist. Thank you.**

**Can't wait to see you.**

**Nobody better turn the lights out,** Marvel says.

**They won't,** I promise. **See you soon.**

She gives me a ☺ but in my mind I can see the real thing.

Thirty minutes later, I climb into my Honda Pilot in my driveway. I wait a moment before starting it. I hold Marvel's gift in my hand and look up into the afternoon sky. It's orange and red and looks like it's been soaking in crystals.

Years ago—so many years when time wasn't a thing—God created all of this from nothing. The daylight and the shimmers and the shadows and the warm glow. He created Marvel, and God created me.

I stare up and hope he can hear me.

"I guess I can't do anything if you take her back."

I feel fear at this sudden realization. All this time I've been fighting to keep her, to make her mine, when Marvel was never mine to begin with.

Tears start to line my cheeks. The wrapped present feels so heavy, like a chunk of Kryptonite in Superman's clutch. I know I'm nervous. And ready. And weary from wondering IF and WHEN and HOW.

"Just give us time. Please, God, give us a little time."

It's a selfish prayer, but I don't know any other kind. Maybe my faith will grow into the sort that will move mountains, but right now I'm struggling with a fragment of faith that is a pale light compared to the splendor of the sky.

# 28

A figure in black walks toward my car, and for a second I really do wonder if it's Marvel. She's in a black coat that comes just to her waist, revealing a short skirt that's really short and long legs that are really long. Her heels have a variety of buckles and straps over her ankles and match the black cap that has the same. Marvel doesn't just look stunning. She looks sexy and grown-up and surely not going out with me tonight.

She smiles and gives me a kiss on the cheek while I stand by her car door like a chauffeur.

"Wow."

That's all I can say. All I need to say.

"Thank you."

She knew this wouldn't be an awesome wave but rather an engulfing tsunami inside of me.

I feel underdressed. Undermatched. Undereverything. I'm wearing black pants and a button-down shirt, but nothing on me screams cool. And the very thought of me being sexy is just stupid. Marvel, on the other hand . . .

"So are we going?" she asks.

"Are you waiting for someone else?" I joke. "I might need to go shopping to buy something that fits with you."

"Stop it. You look handsome, as always."

"You look like a red carpet," I say.

Marvel gives me a perplexed look, and then I realize what I said.

"I mean—you look like you should be walking on the red carpet," I say. "See—I'm having a hard time speaking."

"I'm keeping you off guard," Marvel says as she climbs into my car. "That's all part of my master plan."

I close the door and exhale.

A part of me feels a bit foolish, sitting in this classy little Italian restaurant in an old house in Geneva. I look like a boy who might be going to his high school homecoming dance, but Marvel looks grown-up. Definitely older and more mature than me. Her black- and gray-striped dress hugs her quite nicely. She has an exotic silver belt on around her tiny waist, and the sleeves on the dress seem longer than the lower portion of it.

"Don't tell me you found that at some thrift store," I say.

Marvel shakes her head as she nibbles on the salad. "No. My aunt bought this for me. It's my birthday present."

"Mine or yours?" I ask. "Remind me to thank her."

Her grin glows as if a chandelier is hanging right above our heads. The waiter comes to fill our water glasses. I imagine us coming back to this place ten years from now. Ten years from now, when we can sit and remember that time on this night when we came and ate Italian food and were too young to order anything special to drink and when she looked more beautiful than ever before.

"Thank you for the playlist," she says.

"Sure."

Those dark eyes study me for a moment. "You seem nervous. Why?"

I've barely touched my salad or bread. I've had three glasses of water and for some reason ordered a huge entrée. I keep looking around while feeling the back of my neck sweating.

"Am I?" I ask, trying to play it off.

"Yes, you are. You know it too. What's up?"

"Maybe it's that dress."

Honestly, that is one thing. It's not a warm and fuzzy sort of thing. It's something that's hot and raging.

"Is it too much?" Marvel asks. "I was wondering that. I've never worn something so short and so tight."

"It's pretty great."

The understatement of the world.

"This is just the outside stuff, all of this," she says, waving a hand over her. "You know that, right?"

"Yeah."

I think of my ex, someone who taught me the whole there's-more-to-someone-than-the-outside looks.

"It's only my birthday, Brandon."

I nod. "I know."

"It's still just like any other day."

I take a bite of my bread and smile.

*Just like any other day.*

The dam inside is really, truly about to burst. But I grin

and count the seconds and try to breathe in and out and control my slowly building panic.

We're almost there.

# 29

When we arrive, I can read Marvel's hesitation and concern and also a bit of anger.

"It's not what you think," I tell her.

"We're at a hotel," she says, facing me in the car. "There's not a lot of other things *to* think."

It took us about half an hour to drive to Oak Brook to the Hyatt Lodge, a massive hotel that I only recently learned I have some connections with.

"We're not spending the night," I say quickly.

"Oh, well, that's good for you to let me know. But actually, that sounds even more insulting."

I realize how that sounded and shake my head. Her voice is a combination of humor and serious. I imagine that the serious tone could become a lot more serious if Marvel thought I was here for the wrong reasons.

"There is no room reserved. No—just—please trust me for a second, okay?"

She nods.

Once we're inside, I wave to the guy behind the counter in the lobby (someone I've already spoken to quite a bit today), and I tell Marvel to close her eyes.

"I'm going to guide you somewhere," I tell her.

"This really does not sound good."

"Are you trusting me?"

"I think so . . ."

"Marvel, look—open your eyes."

Those beautiful eyes, curious and excited and nervous, look into mine. I can only imagine what mine look like.

"I love you," I tell her. "Trust me."

"Okay."

I guide her down one long hallway and into another and then I get to the door and open it, making sure she still has her eyes closed. Soon we're standing in the room I've spent considerable time in today.

"You can open your eyes."

Marvel stands and moves her head one way, then the other, then in front of us to see a swimming pool that looks like the sky painted with red and white stars. Her lips open slightly, but she can't say anything. She looks at me, shaking her head, then looks around again.

The surprise covering her is really and truly priceless.

"What is this?"

I smile. "*This* is your lovely day."

She looks confused. "I don't understand."

"Good. 'Cause you usually understand everything a lot more than me."

She moves closer to the pool. There are rose petals scattered all across it, clumps of petals hanging together like berry patches in the middle of the woods. They haven't really moved since Frankie, Barton, and I put them down earlier this afternoon (something I very much wish I had recorded to show Marvel). A cute little rowboat is tied at the edge of the pool.

"What are you—?"

I put a finger on my lips. Marvel's eyes are wide open. She looks at me.

"Brandon, I—"

"Shh," I tell her.

I take off my coat and then help her do the same, since it's warm in this large room. She hands me her cap as well, her dark locks framing her round face. It's funny to see how tall she is in those heels. It's strange to see someone so dressed up and stunning standing in a place where little kids normally run around in their swimsuits. I take her hand and guide her to the edge of the pool, hearing the clicks of her shoes.

"I'm sorry, but I didn't bring my bathing suit," Marvel says.

"You won't be getting wet. Well, let's hope not."

The ceiling of the pool area has glass panels much like the walls around us. All of them are dark, with the night above us and the lights turned off on the sides.

"How did you—?"

"Not now," I say.

"What?"

"You know something? You've been talking ever since you came into my life. You know that?"

A playful, loving glance shines back at me. "And that's a bad thing?"

"Don't talk. For a few moments."

"Is that a real boat?" she asks.

"Yes. And this is that lake in the middle of the summer in a faraway place where nobody else can bother you."

She smiles, maybe knowing.

*No, she thinks this is just a date on her eighteenth birthday and something special but she doesn't know.*

I know that I will never forget this night and that smile and the warm, humid blanket surrounding us. I hold the rowboat and then nod for her to get in. She gracefully climbs into the wobbling thing, holding the stair rail that the boat is tied to with one hand and with the other leaning on my shoulder. She manages to climb in even with those heels. Her dress simply moves with her, sliding up a bit as she sits and before she can adjust it.

I don't do as graceful a job getting into the rowboat. It's the classic kind, one with the oars attached. Eventually I'll have to tell her how I got all this stuff. It'll be fun to tell her, but that's a story for another day. Tonight there's another tale to tell.

I start to row slowly through the red and white petals.

"Where—and how—did you get all these?" Marvel asks.

"Let's just be here and imagine that we're not here, okay?"

Marvel nods and finally yields to my dream. To this perfect day.

"Someone told me that red and white roses together signify unity," I say as we slowly drift to the center of the pool.

Marvel looks over my shoulder toward the door we came through.

"What is Barton doing here?" she asks.

I roll my eyes. He was supposed to wait until her head was facing the other way.

"You must be seeing things."

I turn and see him duck and then bolt back out of the pool area. I laugh. It doesn't matter if this is amateur hour. It's still pretty spectacular.

A piano begins to play, the sound barely loud enough to be heard over our voices.

"Is that music?" she asks.

I nod. Thankfully Barton managed to get the iPod and Bose portable speaker to work. The instrumental sound of Sleeping at Last hovers around us.

Now it's Frankie's turn.

The lights go out, and the ceiling is covered with stars. Well, not really stars but more like disco ball lights. But that's okay. They're coming from two sides of the pool area, a blast of yellow and orange flickering dots.

There are still a handful of emergency lights surrounding us, so a glimmer hovers around us, allowing me to see her perfectly.

"You are crazy," Marvel says.

"Yes, I am, and I think I always will be whenever I'm near you."

"Stop."

So I do as she tells me and stop rowing. We rest in the center, patches of petals gliding on the surface of the water. I realize that this feeling of floating has been there ever since she first entered my life.

"How'd you do this?"

I shake my head as I sit facing her. I move closer and slip my hands around her velvet legs, pulling her toward me.

"Let me look at you," I say. "Okay?"

Her eyes look away. I move my head low enough to glance up at her so she can see me while I talk.

"You are beautiful because your smile lets me see into your soul. You know that? And I'm a little breathless every single time I see it. It's warmer than the sun and it's better and brighter because it really makes me feel alive."

With her confidence back, Marvel shows me more of her soul. "Goodness, Brandon Jeffrey. You are certainly full of words tonight."

"I'll never have enough for you, Marvel. Never."

She grows a little more serious for a moment, maybe knowing now. I don't know.

I still hold her while I start to try and tell her all the things I've rehearsed.

"I believe every word you tell me and always have. About you. About your future. But I belong to you, Marvel. I belong to this sun, moon, and stars that you carry around with you. I want this graceful life. Your peace, the way you are so Zen. Your goodness."

"Brandon, why are you—? Stop this. You're—it's too much. I'm not all that."

I reach into my pocket and grab the wrapped box. Then I smile and feel tears fill my eyes.

"You're more than that and more than I'll ever realize," I say. "But I want to know before it's too late. So here." I hand her the present. "Happy birthday."

She knows now as she pulls off the wrapping, her amazement and amusement tied together in her expression.

"I believe God can answer prayers now," I say. "I believe he can do miracles."

Marvel opens the box and sees the ring inside.

"Marrying me wouldn't be a miracle," she says.

"No. I know. It's having—*keeping*—you around. For as long as I take in breaths and see the sky and know that the world is still halfway decent. 'Cause you're in it."

"Brandon—"

"Marry me."

She shakes her head, her eyes studying the ring. "You're joking."

"I'm as serious as you are and always have been. Marry me. Marry me and let's change God's plan somehow. He can change his mind. He can do what he wants. And maybe he will see something good here. Something good in the two of us just trying to make our way in this black, brutal world. Two scarred and scared people loving each other the way it's supposed to be."

Marvel wipes her eyes and breathes in and smiles once again and then takes the ring.

"Okay," she says.

"I know that maybe there's going to be time for—"

"Shush," she says. "Enough."

Marvel pulls me close and she kisses my lips in the center of hundreds of crimson and ivory petals sleeping on the surface of the water. I think this might be a dream, but then I know it's one I helped create.

She's a dream of someone I wanted to believe existed

but couldn't imagine would smile right through my solitary doorway.

"I don't know what to do about you," Marvel tells me as she slips the ring over her finger.

"I know what to do about you."

I kiss her again and know that maybe there's still time. Maybe there's still hope. Maybe I can keep her from death. At least for a while. At least for the next eighty or ninety years.

# 30

Everybody helped me out with the proposal. I had a lot—and I mean *a lot*—of assistance pulling it all together.

The rowboat I borrowed came from a guy Phil knows, someone who goes fishing a lot and has several different crafts. Frankie, Barton, and I used the trailer I transport my lawn mower in the summertime to haul the rowboat. Barton's parents knew one of the top guys over at the hotel in Oak Brook. Turns out they've stayed there a lot, have gone to various functions there including New Year's Eve outings. They told the manager what I had dreamt up, and they also told him that I was best friends with Devon Teed, the student who was murdered last year by the uncle of the girl I was going to propose to.

People paid for various things—all those rose petals, the rental of the lights—but I did buy the ring myself. It was over $2,500. I'd managed to save quite a bit since last summer. It was supposed to go toward college, of course, but that didn't matter to me anymore. I would've spent double if I could.

It seems like it was seconds ago I fell asleep after kissing Marvel good-bye. Everything in me wanted to stay at the hotel, or to stay in the car, or to stay somewhere on this night. The way she looked and smelled and felt—I think it would have been easy for something to happen. But we had waited this long, and Marvel didn't change. She didn't want to follow something so right with something so wrong. I think I dreamt of her, remembering every single inch of her.

The next morning, the guys and I drop off the boat and then head back to the car. I'm about to open the door when I see someone at the edge of the driveway, standing there facing me on the street. He's tall and has a thick head of hair and he's just standing there as if he's waiting for me.

The morning is gray with fog, and I have to squint to see the guy clearly. When I do, I wish I'd just gotten in the car.

It's Devon. He's standing there in the same tall and slightly awkward pose I remember so clearly. I shut my eyes, knowing I'm not really seeing this. I climb into the Honda and start it up quickly.

"What's your hurry?" Frankie asks in the seat next to me.

"Nothing."

I pull out of the driveway and look all around.

"Who're you looking for?" Barton asks.

"Nobody."

Two blocks farther, I see him again. Standing by the stop sign, just staring at us. I can't breathe. I slow down and look his way. I want to ask the guys if they see him, but I know they don't. This is another one of those *things*. It's not a dream, but it's just—I'm seeing something and I don't understand it.

*Like the time everybody disappeared at Lolla.*

That was one of them. Or the time I saw lights in the sky with Marvel.

I blink, close my eyes, push on the gas pedal, and head back toward Appleton.

The guys talk and joke about last night, laughing especially about the moment Marvel spotted Barton and he dived behind a chair. I was laughing earlier with them, still feeling full and ecstatic from the night before, but now my mood is beginning to resemble the weather around us. Overcast and chilly. Gloomy.

"What's up?" Frankie eventually asks.

"I'm just tired," I say.

This is true, but not the reason I'm suddenly quiet.

"He misses his lady love," Barton says.

"Did you guys talk about the date yet?" Frankie asks.

I nod. "Yeah. Once Marvel got over the surprise and tried to actually imagine doing it, we came up with a date. Or at least I did. Easter. April 21."

"You aren't even waiting for the summer?" Barton says behind me. "Man, you really can't wait to get it on, can you?"

I ignore his comment, even though there's a part of me that agrees with him. But the timing has nothing to do with *that*. It has everything to do with being with Marvel before the end of the school year. Before graduation D-day. I still believe—I *have* to believe—that maybe in some way this will change things. I don't know if Marvel believes that, but the reality hadn't sunk in yet. My random fun idea that winter night while we sat outside had been just that—random and fun to think about. But the ring and the proposal were real. So is the date.

They ask about a few more details and I start to tell them, but then I see Devon on a street corner again. Just looking at me. Not in a sad way or creepy way, but with a serious look. The kind he had when he was talking about the bad things happening in Appleton, about the old guy named Otis, who lives in the quarry, and Jeremy Simmons, the guy he was buying drugs from.

"You're spacing out," Frankie says, staring at me.

"I know. It's just—"

"The man got engaged last night," Barton says. "Give him a break."

*Yeah, and I'm also seeing our dead best friend standing on the curb.*

I need to drop the guys off and then take some Advil or something stronger. Maybe go to sleep.

Soon I'm telling them thanks again and how much I owe them as I drop them off at Barton's house. I claim to have a headache and also say I'm going to be seeing Marvel later today. All of which is true, but honestly, I'm a bit freaked out. Or maybe a lot freaked out. I don't know if I'm truly losing my mind or if I can see dead people like the kid in *The Sixth Sense* or if something else is happening.

I decide to head over to the record store and see if Harry is around. He'll want to know how the night went, so I need to tell him that. But also—being around him gives me a lot of comfort. Much like being around Marvel, but in a different way. There's just something reassuring about having him there.

*Maybe you can tell him about these visions.*

No. I'm not ready for that. But at least maybe they'll go away for a while.

I head down the street that takes me to the record store. And that's when I see them. Not Devon, but all of them.

The sidewalks are lined with people as if they're waiting for a parade. Yet as I pass, I see so many weeping. Couples huddled together, arms around one another, hands held together.

*What's happening here?*

Then I see Devon again, this time in the middle of the crowd, his serious expression mirroring so many others.

I slow down and try to roll down my window, but I can't.

A woman has her face buried in her hands.

A young girl is sobbing, tears dripping off her cheeks.

An older couple looks shell-shocked.

The center of the town is lined with all these people. I drive slowly and wonder how in the world to get out of this nightmare. Are all these people dead? Are they ghosts? They certainly look like it.

Then at the very end I spot one that's definitely not a ghost. It's Marvel. She looks so different from last night. Pale and upset and hurting. I stop the car and try to get out, but I can't. I almost rip the handle of my door, screaming at her, pounding the window, trying to get out to help her.

"Marvel!"

Somewhere between the pounding and the screaming, I look again and she's gone. They're all gone. The sidewalks are empty.

A horn blares at me from behind. I look in the mirror and see the driver shouting at me. I drive on.

**GLORY**

    I don't know where I'm headed anymore. I'm too woozy to even think about going somewhere. I need to just drive a little more and hopefully not see anything else.

    Nothing comes, thankfully. But that doesn't change my mood.

# 31

**Want a free Mexican dinner?**

The text comes at lunch on Monday, two days after I proposed to Marvel. It's from Nick Hamilton, the detective I hired to try to find Devon. He found him, all right. Dead and hidden in a concrete mixer. He also found me. In several different ways.

**Sure**, I text back. I'm not working tonight and don't have any plans. I wonder if he has any new information on anything. Uncle Carlos's whereabouts. Or my father's.

**6:00? At Julio's Tacos in Aurora?**

It's the same place I remember meeting him not long ago. I wonder if he's going to look like he just woke up by the Fox River sleeping off a long night.

**Sure that works**, I write.

I tell Marvel about the dinner before I go. I say I'll stop by and see her afterward, especially since I'll be so close to their apartment. It's nice to be able to tell each other our schedules and where we'll be. Just to make sure we both know. Just in case something weird happens.

I arrive at the restaurant right on time and have to wait fifteen minutes before Nick shows up. His forehead is sweaty and he seems jittery and anxious as he greets me and shakes my hand. Noticing his puffy face and the lines under his eyes, I think he actually looks worse than the last time I saw him. The server leads us to a booth, and Nick doesn't waste any time ordering a margarita.

"How's it going, buddy?" he asks, staring around the restaurant.

"Okay. How are you?"

I'm suddenly a lot more nervous than I was half an hour ago. Nick looks like he's in trouble. He also looks like he's been coping by drinking. I know that look. I know it well.

He shakes his head over and over again, saying he's fine. He guzzles down the water in front of him, then proceeds to do the same once his drink arrives.

"Look, I just wanted to meet you, to see if you knew anything," Nick says. "Have the cops talked to you anymore? Anything about Uncle Carlos?"

"No. What about you?"

Nick curses, looks around the room again, rubs the back of his neck. "The police aren't talking to me at all. They're pissed, to be honest. They think I went around them and made them look foolish. I've even heard some talk that they half blame me for your friend's death."

"How could that be the case?"

"I made them look bad, I guess. In the media. By helping

discover what happened with Devon. By saving your life. And by letting Señor Carlos get away."

"They blame you for all that?"

He scratches at the scruff on his face. "It's just talk. They're not saying I was the reason. But they're sure not sharing anything with me. And I swear, man—I feel watched. I feel—it's worse than ever."

"Watched by who? By the police?"

"I don't know. I told you—the whole thing with Otis—when I was investigating him and he decided to start making my life go to hell. I just think—I think he might be pushing back a little. Anonymously, of course. It's just a hunch."

Nick even seems to be breathing faster. He really looks like things are not so great for him.

"Why do you think that?" I ask. "About Otis?"

"Stuff with my wife—she's divorcing me, getting our kids involved, it's ugly. She knows things—I don't know how. I mean—you make mistakes. Men make mistakes. You're a guy, and you're gonna mess up. That's just it. You will mess up, trust me. And it's just—how she knows some of the stuff, I just don't know."

I doubt that Nick Hamilton is going to be giving any motivational speeches anytime soon. Especially to young men.

"Otis filed a restraining order against me," I tell him.

He curses loud enough to get some looks from other people in the restaurant. "Are you kidding? When?"

"Not long ago. Month or so."

"Why? What prompted it?" Nick asks.

"Nothing. I just—"

"He's setting something up. Just you watch. I told you, Brandon. You don't want to mess around with this guy. You don't."

"I didn't do anything."

"It's tied together—all of it—every little bit. The deaths. Uncle Carlos. This rabbit trail of sorts with the drugs. Otis and the quarry. I've got a file full of weird stuff."

A server interrupts us and takes our order. Nick orders the everything-on-the-menu platter. Judging by how his shirt looks a size too small on his round chest and gut, I think he still loves to eat. A couple of tacos sounds like enough for me.

"What weird stuff are you talking about?" I ask.

"The less you know the better," Nick says, now eating the ice cubes from his drained margarita. "But have you noticed—certain things around here—they're getting weirder. And I'm not just talking about the deaths. I'm just talking—stuff. The mind-sets of kids, parents too."

I'm not sure what he's talking about, but I do think back to Greg and the students terrorizing Seth. The dogs attacking him in the pasture. Tying him to a gravestone. These aren't fun, harmless pranks. They really seem to be *weird*, like Nick is talking about.

*"There is an evil in this world that doesn't blink and doesn't sleep and doesn't feel bad. Ever."*

I remember Nick telling me that at this very restaurant.

"Are you into conspiracies?" Nick asks me.

"No, not really."

If Devon were here, he'd love to talk about conspiracies. There were few of them he didn't believe in.

"You ever hear of a thing called the Illuminati?"

I actually laugh. I know it's sorta an ongoing joke in pop culture. Everybody—especially musicians—are supposedly members of the Illuminati. Secret societies that rule the world and probably perform weird sacrifices.

"I've heard people joke about it."

"Yeah, yeah, I know," Nick says. "I'm just saying—that's the vibe I get. I don't know anything about them—if they're even real. But I know Otis is real. Carlos Acosta—he's real, too. Why the dead kids? Really? Why?"

I shake my head. "So you're saying that Otis—?"

"I'm telling you that *something*—I don't know what, but something—is going on. Bigger than just a random death. Bigger than some Mexican killing a couple of kids."

I think back to the warehouse on Rush Street in Appleton and about Otis and Carlos meeting there. About what I saw in there, or at least what I barely saw in the darkness before being run off. About how they emptied everything out of there like Sergeant Harden said. I don't say this to Nick, because there's nothing to say. Devon might have had a few thoughts and theories, but I don't.

Nick orders another drink and then devours the food once it arrives. He asks a few questions about me and about school and Marvel, and I answer them in brief sentences. I don't tell him much. I certainly don't mention that I'm going to marry Marvel. I still don't really know this guy. I don't really trust him either.

"Carlos worries me," Nick says after he's licked his plate clean. "The other stuff I'm talking about—that's just—I don't know, maybe it's nonsense. My soon-to-be ex told me not long ago that I was crazy. *Delusional* was the actual word she used. Said that my drinking was causing my brain to go to pot. But that's the irony. I think it's because I've lightened up and done some investigating—because I've actually been brave and stupid enough to go down that road—that I've discovered things. She doesn't realize—it basically scares me. I gotta have a way to cope. We all do."

"My father likes to cope that way too," I say, not trying to be mean but unable to *not* say anything.

"Yeah, I know. I'm not that kind of guy."

*I bet that's what Dad once told himself.*

"You—your pretty little girlfriend—I know the cops still keep tabs on her. But this Carlos. I don't think he's split to another state. I think he's still out there. I'm looking too. I just don't have any leads. So anything you find out, you tell me. Okay?"

I nod.

"Anything," he continues, draining his glass. "Any weird thing, any vibe, anything you see that just doesn't feel right. You got it? Text me. Anytime. God knows it's not like I'm busy taking the kids to the zoo or making waffles for my wife."

He adds a frustrated curse to that last thought.

"I'll let you know," I tell him.

I'm not lying, either. I will simply be selective on the things I decide to share with Nick. He's still more like my father than like Harry. And regardless of the fact that he pulled me out of Lake Michigan one night not long ago, I wonder if he's in any condition to do that again.

Maybe Nick needs to pull himself out of the dark waters.

# 32

An hour later I find myself tucked in Marvel's bedroom, lying next to her on the small bed while her laptop streams music. Her head is resting on my chest, her oversize sweatshirt looking like a blanket covering her. Her aunt's cousin greeted me when I arrived—a friendly, smiling woman in her late twenties or early thirties who doesn't speak much English and doesn't seem to have any idea who I might be. Marvel told her in Spanish a little bit about me. She nodded and disappeared.

"I love these guys," Marvel says.

A woman is singing a soft song about God and light and avalanches and love.

"Who is it?"

"Hillsong United."

"Some of these songs sound all the same," I say. "They're all saying the same thing."

"Well, in a way, there really is only one thing to say, you know?" Marvel says in a similar soft voice. "People are lost, and God finds us. He loves us. He saves us. It's the same story that never gets old."

I think about her words. It's not that I don't believe her. I do. I know that God saved me, that I trusted him, that things changed for me. Somehow. I can feel it deep down. But I'm still unsure what to do now. Where to go with that. Occasionally I feel inspired and motivated, and other times I feel totally unsure. Like the candle's been blown out and I'm just seeing all the bad stuff in the world again, feeling kind of hopeless.

"You okay?" Marvel asks. She shifts and turns to rest on one elbow and face me.

"Yeah. Just thinking about what you said. And about the dinner I had with Nick. And about sort of everything. I just want to go back to the other night. To be with you."

"You're here with me now," Marvel says. "I'm just not wearing a skirt."

I laugh. "Stop. It's not that. Well, maybe it's a little of that. No. It's just . . . I so wish I had that. Those feelings you have inside. That belief."

"They don't just come overnight." Marvel brushes her hair away from her face. "I found faith a lot earlier than some people do. Some people never find it. You know?"

"Yeah."

"Some people spend their whole lives hoping to hear from God. And they don't. So I remind myself how blessed I am."

I nod, but I can't help thinking that maybe you don't want to hear from God if what he's going to tell you is that one day soon you'll die.

This guest bedroom is mostly bare, blank walls and

just a bed and a desk. An ornate gold cross the size of my hand hangs on the wall over the bed. Marvel has a couple of suitcases on the floor with clothes that haven't even been unpacked. It would feel drab if Marvel wasn't filling this place with her bright rainbow of colors.

"Are we rushing things?" Marvel asks me.

I stare down and study her lips carefully. I shake my head with a confident no.

"Seriously," she says. "I don't know."

"I do."

"What did your mom say?"

"At first she told me I was crazy," I say. "Too young, too broke, too dumb, too much of a guy. But I told her that I've had a pretty normal life with a pretty screwed-up father, and the most amazing thing shows up out of nowhere and I love her. She didn't have much of an answer for that."

"My aunt is angry with me."

"She doesn't get to have a say. Nobody does. We're both eighteen."

Marvel sits up to face me. "I know. I'm just talking about you and me. Yes, we're eighteen. But, Brandon—we are *eighteen*."

"Things are also a little more unique with us."

"I just want to do the right thing. Usually—I know it's good to pray over things—and this was such a surprise."

"Does it feel wrong to you?" I ask.

"No." Her eyes look at me and through me, studying me until she moves closer and kisses me. "No, it doesn't feel wrong."

Eyes closed, I sink into her and feel like I'm hovering over this small house and this town and this place. We're flying and as long as I clutch her with hands that need her and don't let go, we'll be fine; everything will be just fine.

"Brandon, okay, easy," Marvel says, pulling back a bit, out of breath.

"I'm sorry."

"It's okay. Just—"

I nod. "Yeah, sorry."

I sigh and start breathing again.

"This keeps getting more and more dangerous," Marvel says.

"What?"

"This. Being here with you. Because I don't want to stop. I don't want you to apologize."

"No, it's fine. I just—some things simply feel right."

Marvel moves and sits on the edge of the bed, still right beside me but not as comfortable as she was a few moments ago.

"You know, Brandon—this isn't some kind of stand I'm trying to make. It's not just the thing that I'm *supposed* to do."

"What do you mean?" I ask.

"By stopping. By not having sex. I've thought a lot about it. A lot. I feel God's been pretty clear. I'm not choosing this because of what some adult or pastor is telling me—it's because of what God's told me. I promised him—I'm his. I feel—I feel if I break that promise, something will change. Maybe that's my imagination, I don't know. But for some reason, he spoke to me. He rescued me. I *want* to obey what he says."

I nod, hearing her, really and truly hearing instead of listening.

"I know I've said it over and over again—"

"It's okay," I tell her, moving so I can sit next to her. I take her hand.

"I'm a broken record."

"Marvel, look—if something happened to me like what happened to you, I'd be calling the news. I'd go on the morning shows and talk shows telling my story. God spoke to you. It wasn't just one of those *I think God's trying to tell me this* sort of things. No. This was like *real*."

"You really believe me?"

I'm surprised to hear her say that, to see the question on her face. "Of course I do. I've told you I do."

"I know, but still. I know how it sounds."

"Did he tell you not to mess around with guys too?" I ask, grabbing her hand and trying to lighten the mood.

"No. I know what the Bible says about purity, and I believe that. But it's like—it's like I'm chosen for this thing and I have to try to do everything I can. To be there. To be guarded, to be able to hear the Spirit. You know? That's such a big thing, you know? Giving myself over to someone."

"Not just anyone," I say.

"You know what I mean."

"I do. And I don't ever mean to pressure you. But that's all I feel. Pressure. I mean—you know, like worrying and all that, not actual—"

She laughs. "You are cute when you blush."

"And babble."

"Yes, that too."

Marvel leans over and kisses me, and as she does, I have this wild sort of realization.

   The God of this universe who made everything and who gave his Son to die for us and who allows us to come before him with all our garbage actually decided to communicate to this girl I've fallen in love with and am connected to.

   *So did you bring her to me?*

   I knew the moment I met Marvel that she was special, but for the first time in like ever, I consider that maybe I'm special too.

# 33

When I see my father, I know that I'm not dreaming.

It's Thursday and I'm not working tonight. I hung out with my fiancée after school for a while (a phrase I'm just loving to say) and got home around six thirty to see if there was anything good for dinner. Marvel and I still haven't told anybody at school about our engagement, and she's decided not to wear the ring. All the girls in school would notice the ring and start asking what's up. My mom and her aunt know, of course. So do people like Harry and Frankie and Barton. I've told them all to keep quiet, and surprisingly even Barton has managed to comply. Eventually we'll tell people. How and when, I'm not sure, but I'm not worried about it.

What I am worried about is walking into an empty house and finding my father waiting for me. Nobody else is around—at least not that I can see or hear—so finding him sitting on the couch is quite a shock.

If it were two days earlier, this could have been the absolute worst April Fools' joke ever.

*April 1, here's the biggest fool in the world coming back home!* But no, it's April 3.

"Hello, Brandon."

These two words inspire a black sort of dread deep inside, like some kind of dark tar. Thick and messy, the kind that gets dumped into an ocean and you can never quite get rid of it.

I can't help but go into defensive panic mode. More than ever before, I have purpose and direction in my life. And it's not just me standing here. It's this family unit, the ones Dad left behind. I'm standing here for them. And I'm standing here for Marvel, too. My girlfriend, my fiancée, my soon-to-be wife. All of this makes me look around quickly for something I can use if necessary to fend my father off. The last time I saw him, I bashed a lamp over his head.

*The coasters.*

There's a set of stainless steel coasters on the cabinet right underneath the flat-screen television on the wall. Most of the time they're just sitting there collecting dust. They could be used like ninja throwing stars. They'd at least slow him down.

Dad just sits there on the couch, watching me. The hard face is clean-shaven, his hair short and combed back. He's wearing clothes that appear to be actually clean and ironed. But more than all of that, it's his eyes that shock me, and not just because they're not blurry and bloodshot. It's their expression. It isn't just apologetic, it's crushed.

Dad stands but remains by the couch, not moving toward me. Maybe he can tell I'm a bit freaked out. He's holding a small wrapped package.

"I'm sorry I missed your birthday. I'm sorry I've missed it for the last few years."

His tone is different. I've never heard him sound like this. At least not that I can remember. He's used that word *sorry* before, but never like this.

"Please, Brandon—take this. I'm going to the cops after I give it to you. To talk to them and to do whatever I have to."

"Does Mom know you're here?" I ask.

I can't help sounding defensive and angry. Maybe even more than I'm feeling. But my whole being is a little bit in shock.

Dad nods. "Yes. She's with the boys at a store."

"Do they know you're here?"

"No. Not yet. I wanted to see you first."

Normally my father has a hard time standing still. Unless, of course, he's watching one of his teams lose while guzzling down beer. But he's standing there, waiting on me to take this gift. I don't have a choice.

The package is light, too light to be much of anything.

"I'm sorry I didn't get you a card. I found a bunch of them that all say stuff that just sounds like bu—" He stops. "I don't want any of this to be phony. I just—I want to figure out how to start over."

I look down at the blue-and-yellow wrapping.

"Go ahead," he says. "Please."

I peel off the paper. Inside is a long white envelope. As I open it, I can see money inside. Hundred-dollar bills. Quite a few of them.

"I've had this bank account—not much—but it was my fly-the-coop stash. When I left you guys, I withdrew it all. I was planning on taking off. But then—well, in the midst of some really bad days and nights—I realized that I'd already been gone a long time."

The cash in my hand feels like it's got a racing heartbeat. I don't know what to do with it.

"Listen, Brandon," he says as I notice deep ruts under his eyes. "I'm not—this isn't like I'm trying to buy you off or anything. I know I don't have a right to give you anything. It's just—that's for you, for your eighteenth birthday. You're a man now. Free to do what you want."

I think of the scar on my right arm, the one he stamped with a hot spatula.

*I want you to get the hell away from me.*

This is what goes through my head, but then I feel guilty for having such a thought. I think back to what Harry told me when I had lunch with him.

*"God's love is powerful enough to get over any wall. He can open anyone's heart and find them. And—thankfully for all of us—forgive them."*

I don't say anything, but I guess that's better than lashing out like a part of me wants to.

"Brandon—I've gotten some help. Some good, honest help with some good people. I know I've said it before and those are just lines, and I'm not expecting you to believe. But I still need you to know that. Okay? I swear that I'll never touch you or your brothers again."

He looks like he wants to say more, but I can tell he's a little wrecked. There are tears in his eyes, and they frighten me. More than almost anything's frightened me my whole life. Dad forces this really sad smile and then he nods, walks past me, and goes out the door.

I don't follow. I can't. I'm numb and afraid.

For the first time in . . . well, maybe ever . . .I realize something.

I've been carrying an iceberg of hate around with me. On the surface, it's bright and small and manageable. But under the surface, where nobody—not even Marvel—can see, it's massive and buried and dark. It's a foundation that I've been resting on for a long time.

I don't think anything can melt it away. Not in some instant.

But I have to believe that maybe God can help me chip away at it.

I want to believe that my father is telling the truth. That maybe he's gotten better. The thought of some feel-good toss-the-football-around laughing-lots confidant sort of relationship is insane. That's never happening. I know that.

But can there be something? Could this really be possible?

Did God's love climb over the steel gates around my father's heart and get his attention?

I'm scared to know the answer. I'm scared to believe it might be true.

# 34

I don't have much of a conversation with my mother when she comes home. I'm angry but not exactly sure what I'm angry about. For Mom not telling me he was going to be there? For Dad not seeing my brothers? For words I wanted to hear (whatever they might be)?

*Maybe you're angry because you can't justify your anger any longer.*

I don't tell Mom about the money he gave me. There's no way I'm keeping it, of course. No way I'm going to spend it on me. But I'm not giving it back to Dad either. Maybe I'll give it to a charity. To Harry and his family. To Marvel and her aunt. Someone somewhere can use his blood money.

"I believe your father can change," Mom tells me before I retreat to my room to try to figure things out. "Anybody can change, Brandon."

Maybe I'm frustrated because this suddenly just shakes my world. Dad being in the picture, whatever picture it might be, changes the color of everything. This freedom and hope I've been carrying around feel deflated.

I just don't know if Dad—and Mom—are right.

*Can he change? Can Dad really and truly change?*

I almost call Marvel, but I decide to wait. I'm full of all this swirling stuff going through my head and heart, so I need to just chill. Do some homework. Go online and see what kind of nonsense is happening.

It's so easy to find my way to Marvel's blog. Waiting there is another gift. It's not wrapped and has no monetary value, but it's like some kind of medicine for my soul.

### HOME

Touching ground in some kind of hideaway

The strands that allow us to stay

Close but so faraway

I long for rest

For a river

For the road heading west

For a place to race home

We keeping heading there but we're still here

We dream but find the rest of the nightmare

We hope

All while you hold my hand

Drifting toward a place called home

Where we can be free

Where we can simply be

Just you and I

At rest at home

It's ironic to be sitting at home and yet feeling like I'm more at home reading these words and being in that world. Marvel's world. She's out there, but right now she's beside me once again.

Home isn't a building or a family. For me, it's Marvel.

# 35

"I need your help."

It's a rare thing to have Seth call me, and even more rare to have him ask me for help.

"What's this about?"

"Jeremy."

I wonder if Jeremy finally caught up with Seth. Maybe he did, and maybe he's holding Seth in handcuffs in his barn asking him to hit him as hard as he can.

*The first rule of fight club is . . .*

"What's going on?" I look around the record store for Phil. He must be in the back somewhere.

"I need to borrow some money."

"What for?"

"So I don't get found floating in the Fox River."

Not too long ago, someone might have said this to me and I'd laugh. Not anymore. The dead seem to be popping up everywhere these days.

"But what's the money for?"

"Do you need to know?" Seth asks.

"Well, yeah, that would sorta be nice."

"What do you think?" he says.

"I know Jeremy, so there's not much to think."

It's some kind of drug. The question is what kind.

"Is this for you?" I ask. I see Phil coming out of the back room.

"Again, why is it so important to know?"

"Because, *again*, this might be a problem."

"There's no problem here," he says. "I need your help."

Phil doesn't have his hair in a ponytail today, so his flowing gray-white locks along with his beard give him a Gandalf look. He picks up a stack of records that just came in. He moves at about five miles an hour. I don't want to say anything that will get his attention. Like *pot* or *crack* or *meth* or *heroin*.

"I don't want you to overdo it."

Seth curses. He usually gets this way after being pushed, and I'm not trying to push. I'm just trying to know what I would be loaning him money for.

"Look, I don't want to get in trouble," I say.

"You won't. This is just a payment. It's not like it's the whole amount. I've got a payment plan going."

"How much are you asking for?"

"Two hundred and fifty bucks."

I laugh. "Hey, I just have it in my pocket. Some extra change."

"You'll get it back. I promise. Look, I know you're a saver."

I'm about to say something about being engaged, about

the upcoming wedding, about my upcoming big major life change. But then I remember the money from my father.

I get an idea.

"Look—did you ever say anything about that night at the farm with Greg and his dogs?" I ask.

"No." Short, quick, blunt response.

I haven't stopped thinking of this, and the more I think about it, the angrier I get.

"If you let Frankie and me go to the cops about it, and to the school, I'll loan you the money."

"No way."

"Okay, fine. No money then."

"Brandon, you don't have to do that. I need the money. Seriously. I was going to borrow some from my folks without telling them, but they took their little stash away recently. I don't know—maybe they had an idea I knew where it was."

Stealing from his parents. Great friend I have here.

"You don't understand—you just let this Greg guy do something awful. And nobody did a thing about it. It's still the big joke everywhere."

"I'm aware of that," he says in a robotic sort of voice. "That's not my problem. My problem is Jeremy. For the time being."

The door opens, and a couple of guys who look like college students come in. I've seen them before. Phil glances back at me, just curious to see if I'm there. I nod to him to let him know I'll get off the phone.

"I gotta go."

"I need that money, Brandon."

"Then let me tell people what happened. I'm sick of Greg. I want him kicked out of school."

There is a pause, and I tell him again I have to go.

"Fine. Go ahead, whatever. Just—can I get that money?"

"When?"

"Tonight."

"What? Like after work?"

"Yeah. Just come in the house. The door is unlocked like always. I don't want my folks asking why someone's coming by. They're already suspicious of me."

I want to ask him why, but I just say I'll see him later. Soon I'm talking to the guys who just walked in, forgetting for the moment about Seth and the money.

Maybe it's a dumb thing to do, to loan it to him. But I don't want my father's money for myself. Maybe for Marvel and me, but I don't even know about that. To give it to someone like Seth—sure, the reasoning might be not the best, but I'm helping out.

All along I've just wanted the guy to get a little help.

As for Greg, I want him to get what he deserves. I haven't forgotten.

# 36

The moon hides behind thick clouds tonight. I park on the curb down the street from Seth's house, then walk up to the door and open it slowly. Just like he said, it's unlocked. I feel like an intruder, but thankfully no dog is by the front to bark out a greeting. I get to the stairs and climb them two at a time. I don't knock at his door but open it and step inside. Seth is on his computer at his desk. He turns and sees me breathing heavily and he just laughs.

"It's not like they'd call the cops on you," Seth says. "Did you bring it?"

"No, I just wanted to see what's up."

I pull the money from my pocket and hand it to him. Something in me tells me not to do this, that this isn't a good decision. But I don't want to find Seth in a ditch somewhere with the imprints of Jeremy's knuckles on his bloody face.

"What are you buying with this?"

"The future," Seth says. "I'm buying the future. Okay?"

"How's that? You planning on dealing?"

He closes his laptop as if he doesn't want me to see what's on it. "Everybody has plans, Brandon."

Seth is wearing a black tank top that shows off his puny arms. I notice a new tattoo on his bicep.

"When'd you get that done?" I ask.

"A month ago."

"Those aren't cheap."

"Jeremy knew a guy. I got it for free."

"Yet you owe Jeremy money?"

"Two very different things."

I examine the image closer. It's some kind of twisting star, maybe the ninja star I've heard Seth talk about. It's black with yellow flames that light its edges.

"What exactly is that?"

He smiles. "I call it my little dancing star."

"Dancing star?" I ask. "You have dreams of going on *Dancing with the Stars*?"

My joke doesn't get a laugh or even a smile.

"Nietzsche said, 'You need chaos in your soul to give birth to a dancing star.'"

Seth quotes the guy with the weird name just like someone quoting a line from their favorite pop song.

"Don't you have enough chaos in your life?" I ask him.

Again, there's no reaction. Sometimes I think that some of the bullying and anger directed at the guy is because he just doesn't give much back. To anybody. Even the guy who is loaning him money in order to keep him from getting beaten up or worse.

"That Neechee guy—you titled the movie you made from a quote of his, right?"

This makes an impression. Seth actually smiles and nods and then opens his computer. It looks like he's in iMovie, working on clips of his video.

"I'm going to upload my movie very soon."

"The abyss one, right?"

"*The Gaze of the Abyss*. But I can't show you right now. It's getting a lot better. I added some more to it."

I hold up my thumb as he shuts the laptop again.

"So Jeremy's going to leave you alone then?"

"Yep."

I glance around the room but don't see any drugs or anything related to drugs—not that I would necessarily recognize it if I saw it. I don't smell the scent of pot anywhere either. Seth doesn't have that stoner look to him. Sometimes it seems like he's somewhere far off in Sethland, but I don't think that's the place where potheads go.

Once again, I think of telling him about Marvel and me, but I don't. Maybe it's because I know he'll shrug it off or even act like he didn't hear me.

*"Everybody has plans."*

Yeah, they do. And often we don't tell many others about those plans. We reveal them only to a select few, possibly out of fear of the plans never actually coming to pass. Or maybe simply because we don't want others to know about the hopes we have.

Seth and I are on very different tracks in life. I still want to help him out. Not like this, with money for drugs, but maybe with friendship. Maybe just to help him the way Marvel and Harry and others have helped me. Maybe just to reach out and offer some tiny bit of hope. We all need it.

# 37

It's been a long time since I've seen Devon's parents. Too long. There have been times when I called and didn't get anybody. Even times when I knocked at their house, knowing someone was home. But the door never opened.

On the way to school I think about how many times Devon drove me there and how I got accustomed to the rides. I miss them.

*No, you miss him.*

So out of the blue, I drive over to his house. There are two cars in the driveway, so I know someone has to be home.

I think back to Devon's funeral. It was over a month ago, but in some ways it feels like a year. A lot has changed since then. Yet there's this empty spot inside me that I think will always be there. Like the mark a gunshot might make. If you survive being shot—*if* being the key word—then you live with that scarred nick in your skin the rest of your life.

For the Teeds, I imagine it's a lot bigger than a nick. More like missing a limb, maybe. Like the left hand mourning the loss of the right one.

I knock and hear a voice inside. When the door opens, I see a skin-and-bones version of Mrs. Teed.

"Brandon. I was just thinking of you. Please, come in."

As I enter the house, I notice the entryway for maybe the first time. Everything is incredibly neat and tidy. I smell some type of lemon cleaner or maybe air freshener. A voice calls from upstairs asking who's there, and Mrs. Teed tells her husband it's me. He doesn't respond. But that's been Mr. Teed as long as I've known him.

"Don't you have school today?" she asks.

"Yeah. I just—I haven't seen you guys in a while. I'm sorry."

She gives me a grim sort of smile. Her eyes are trying to look bright, but they only look tired. She reminds me of the way the people look on *Survivor* after forty days in some remote location.

"You don't need to apologize. I've been meaning to call you. How are you doing?"

"Good."

Good seems to be a proper middle ground between the awful stuff at home and with Uncle Carlos and the amazing stuff happening with Marvel.

"I heard about your father," she says.

I nod and glance up the stairs heading away from the entryway. "Yeah, I think most people have."

"I saw him recently."

"Really?" I ask, surprised. "Where?"

"At our church. We've been going to an amazing program

called Celebrate Recovery. It's for all types of people, not just those with addictions, but anyone who's hurting. I've seen your father there. I shouldn't tell you that, actually, but . . . this is an unusual case."

So Dad was telling the truth. He's really trying.

"Yeah, he came by. Spoke to me."

"Can I tell you something, Brandon?"

Her haunting glance makes me want to dart back out of the house. I'm suddenly afraid of what she might say or that she's going to break down in front of me.

"Yeah."

"I know some of what's happened in the past. Devon told me a few things in confidence, because he was scared for you. I never told anyone else. But it's not like we didn't know how rough things had gotten, with your dad's drinking."

I look away, wondering how this suddenly became about me.

"Brandon—he's the only father you'll ever have. I know something—none of us is promised tomorrow. God allows things to happen that don't make sense. Awful things. It's because this world is fallen and because we're all sinners. But that doesn't mean we can't change. It doesn't mean we can't give those hurts and habits over to God. Or at least try to, every day."

Seeing the new Mrs. Teed and hearing her tone that sounds so different from what it used to be, I know she's speaking from the heart. I want to believe she's right too. I nod again.

"There's not an hour that goes by that I don't think of

Devon. The only way we've been able to cope is through God's power. He can help you too."

"I know that," I tell her.

And I do know. I believe this. It's just there's a whole other part of me that's full of bad stuff that doesn't want to know and doesn't want to believe. That only wants to lash out because of all the hurt inside.

"I better head to school," I tell her. "I just wanted to say hi."

"Thank you," Mrs. Teed says. "Please stop by and say hello anytime. I'm praying for you and your family, Brandon."

"Okay," I say, then tell her I'm doing the same.

I need to *start* doing the same. Praying.

Yeah. I need to do more of that.

If God can hear those prayers, then I'm really lucky. Then we're really lucky.

I know he doesn't answer all of them. But he might answer a few.

# 38

When I first told Mom about my grand plan with Marvel, she laughed. It made me feel very juvenile and very stupid until she took my hand and apologized.

"I haven't ever seen you this way," she told me.

"What way?" I asked.

"So romantic."

Of course she tried to convince me I was indeed acting juvenile and stupid. Where would we live and what would we do after high school graduation and what about college and finding jobs? I kept telling her I didn't have all the answers and then asked her if she had all the answers when it came to Dad. I wasn't trying to be mean, just trying to compare the situations. This made her stop telling me I was crazy.

But she did end up asking an obvious parent question.

"Tell me, Brandon. Is Marvel pregnant?"

I could only shake my head. "Yes. We just found out she's carrying twins. I'm naming them Alex and Carter."

"Very funny," Mom said. She couldn't hide her obvious relief.

There were a lot of details I hadn't thought of, it's true, and the more we talked, the more Mom offered to help us. The more it seemed she really *wanted* to help.

The first and most obvious question was where this wedding would take place. Easter Sunday falls on April 21 this year, so we plan to have an Easter wedding reception at my house. One day earlier, Marvel and I will head to the Kane County clerk to get a wedding license. Maybe someday in the future we'll have one of those big weddings in the church where everybody will line the pews and afterward we'll head to some fancy banquet hall for a night of eating and dancing and fun. But we're eighteen and still in high school, so we have limited choices.

Over lunch one day Marvel tells me, "I want a pastor to conduct a ceremony."

"I thought we'd decided to go to the courthouse to make it official."

"I know," Marvel says. "But official in the eyes of Illinois isn't official in the eyes of God."

"Really?"

She laughs. "Why do you think they have wedding ceremonies? It's about pledging ourselves to one another. Not just before some guy working for the county, but before God. Making our promises to him. That's why you do it. And that's something we have to do."

"So can we do this at my house? My mom actually suggested it. To have a small ceremony and then a reception. Or luncheon, as you keep calling it."

"That's a great idea."

"You know who would be great to officiate?" I say. "Harry. Wouldn't that be awesome?"

"I don't think he's an ordained minister."

I drain my can of Coke. "Details. Come on."

"What did he say about your plans?" she asks.

"*My* plans? These are *our* plans. At first I could tell he was surprised. He didn't say anything. Well, he did say something about what a big step marriage is. But then he said congratulations and joked that we owe him for bringing us together."

"We do," Marvel says. "I know that a pastor—whoever we use—will want to talk to us. To give us counsel. They're not just going to come off the street and marry us."

"Is there an app to find some preacher for that?" I joke.

"There's an app for everything, so yes, I'm sure there is."

We only have a few minutes before next period.

"Can you believe it?" I ask her. "You and me getting married?"

"No, I can't. But every morning when I wake up, it's the first thing I think about. And the last thing before I fall asleep. And not once have I felt God telling me not to do this."

"Can I ask you something?"

She looks perplexed. "Of course."

"Have you had any more dreams? Or visions? Or anything?"

"No," she says. "Not recently."

"Maybe that's a good thing, you know?" I say.

"Yes. Maybe it is."

"Maybe the bad stuff that's happened is behind us," I say.

"Maybe somehow you already did what you needed to do. Have you thought about that?"

She nods and then glances around the cafeteria. "I have. But I don't think that's the case."

I want to say more, to tell her things I've already said, to suggest that our coming together and discovering what happened with Uncle Carlos might change the future. Maybe getting married will change things. Maybe the prayers will.

There are so many maybes that I want to remind her about. But she already knows them.

"I hope Easter is a sunny day," I tell her.

"It will be. Every Easter is a glorious day to celebrate."

There she goes again, putting things in that other perspective. I smile and nod and agree with her.

This will be the first *real* Easter I get to celebrate. And I'll be doing it in quite the extraordinary way.

# 39

All I see are eyes in the shadows, fiery red and watching in the night.

I hear quick, restless breathing, like some kind of rabid dog chained and trying to get out of its cage. No, not a cage, a room. There's scratching at a sliding-glass door.

The rage and the hate press against me, pushing me up against the wall. I feel like I'm being smothered by a crowd. I'm dizzy and out of breath and try to fight my way through to see more.

The scratching and the breathing grow louder and faster. Then I feel the hot, sick panting against my face. The smell—the wet feel—and those eyes.

Then it laughs. He laughs. I recognize the sound and know that I'm in danger. Marvel is in danger. We've waited too long. We've forgotten. We've neglected the monster staring us in the face and waiting to attack.

The figure, monstrous and hulking, like something out of *The Lord of the Rings*, turns and strikes. The window breaks and glass shatters and crumbles to the ground. The monster keeps laughing, howling, and then it leaps out to the world.

I'm left shaking, my hands groping in the dark, trying to find the exit, trying to warn the others, trying to get to Marvel. But I can't breathe. My legs are locked. And this black cell I'm in only grows darker.

I scream and fumble in the shadows and try to hold on to something.

"Brandon! Hey, Brandon, wake up, Brandon—"

The shouts and the shaking come from Alex. He's sitting on the edge of my bed, in my room, in our house, in our neighborhood. I can see the glow of my computer on my desk.

"Sounds like a pretty bad one," Alex says.

I sit up and wipe my forehead. It feels like I've been working out.

"What were you dreaming about?"

I try to catch my breath. I can only shake my head. "I don't know," I say.

I get this awful feeling, another one to add to the whole lot full of them. I see my brother's face, concerned and wanting to help. I blink and see that face motionless, eyes shut, the way it would look in a casket . . .

*God, no. Brandon, stop it now.*

"Brandon? What's wrong?"

"Nothing," I force myself to say. "Nothing. Just—thanks. I'm okay."

"Sure?"

"Listen to you." I'm trying to sound like myself. Trying hard. "Listen to you taking care of big brother."

He just shrugs like it's part of the deal. We're there and we take care of each other.

"Go back to sleep. I'm fine."

"Okay," Alex says, slipping back out of my room.

My room feels normal, just like always, but I blink and see those red eyes again. Then I blink again and see the eyes of my brother. Shut. And locked forever.

# 40

"There's gonna be a blood moon tonight," Phil tells me.

It's the first week of April and everybody's buzzing about the lunar eclipse that's supposed to occur.

"Does that mean you're gonna turn into a werewolf tonight?" I ask.

"Nope," Phil says. "I only do that every third Thursday."

It's unusual having Phil, Harry, and me all at Fascination Street at once, but this week is busy as we gear up for Record Store Day this coming Saturday. It's a day where the store does quite a bit of its yearly business.

Harry is more serious than usual, and I know it's because he's anxious about the big day. He's in the back doing something. I'm putting items on sale that he listed out on a computer sheet. Pink Floyd's classic album is playing—Phil's choice because of the blood moon.

"We should've had Dennis Shore back in for a book signing," Phil says. "A *Dark Side of the Moon* signing."

Harry is walking toward me and overhears. "He told

me last time he was in that he's gonna try his hand at some nonfiction."

"Yeah?" Phil asks. "What about?"

"A book on demons. He didn't get too specific. Just said there were some things he'd heard about in North Carolina. Like some spooky town that was in the news not long ago. And a story about some missionary couple who experienced some demonic attacks. He wanted to know more—to see if they were connected."

For Harry to mention this now of all times—the day after I had that awful nightmare about the demon eyes . . . I can't help but ask.

"Are demons real? I mean—I know they're real. But are they like real people or what? The movies always have them either as these weird winged things or stuck inside small children."

Harry pauses at the counter and reflects. "Oh, they're real. What they look like, I'm not sure. What do angels look like? Not the kind in films or on Hallmark cards. The Bible says angels are beautiful beings and demons happen to be the fallen ones. But angels and demons can take on different appearances. I believe there are angels in our midst that we never know about."

Phil watches us as if he might have some thoughts, but he doesn't share.

"If you believe in God, can demons hurt you?" I ask.

Harry scratches his beard, which has grown thicker than usual. "Of course. Well, let me rephrase that. We're told that we're literally fighting them. And they're coming against us daily in every way possible. Not just in big ways, but in the small ones. Discouragement, isolation, pride . . . Life as a believer is a daily battle."

I nod but probably don't give him the most optimistic look. Harry sees my expression and seems to understand the things inside me. Curiosity, maybe. Doubt, certainly. Fear, obviously.

"You know, there's a version of the Bible called *The Message*," he says. "It makes Scripture a lot easier to understand. There's a verse I love that says something to the effect that you need to yell a loud *No* to the devil, then watch him scurry away. You need to say a quiet *Yes* to God and he'll come quickly. I think of that 'cause it seems like I'm saying that *No* all the time."

The song changes into a slow, dreamy ballad. Phil wanders over to us with a weird sort of grin on his face.

"Remember, boys, 'We are not fighting against flesh-and-blood enemies, but against evil rulers and authorities of the unseen world, against mighty powers in this dark world, and against evil spirits in the heavenly places.'" He nods as if telling himself, *That's right*. "Rulers. Authorities. *Mighty spirits*. That's all. Such an easy task, right?"

He laughs as the singer hums through the speakers about "us and them."

"For *them* it's a blood moon every night," Phil tells us. "For them, the eclipse is eternal. Their shadows look bright now, but just wait. Just you wait."

The grim bearded prophet heads back over to what he was doing. Harry looks at me and raises his eyebrows and widens his eyes. Then he smiles. I know he loves Phil and maybe he even believes in what he just said, but that doesn't mean he can't joke about Phil being so *Phil*.

*The end is near, man. It's groovy, so let's turn up the classic rock.*

"Just to be on the safe side, I'd avoid picking up any hitchhikers tonight," Harry tells me.

His advice lingers in the air like famous last words.

# 41

About four seconds after I climb into the Honda Pilot and turn the key, I know something's wrong. I hear a sound behind me, and just as I turn my head, a gloved hand cups my mouth and nose and presses hard. A knife pricks the side of my throat.

"I want you to drive down to the quarry," says a familiar voice.

Marvel's missing uncle Carlos is no longer missing.

"You do what I say or I'll kill you right this very second," he says in a controlled voice. "I'm going to kill you anyway, but it's your choice how long I wait to do it."

My body is basically frozen, and he has to prick me again with the knife before I pull the car out onto the street. Nobody is around.

"Drive," he says.

I follow his order. I wonder if we're going to see Otis Sykes. I wonder if I'm finally going to know what's really happening with the two of them. Before I die.

Moments later, I park the vehicle and shut off the engine, giving him the keys as he asks. I'm sweating and numb and everything inside me is on pause. I'm waiting. Watching for anything to do or say. Afraid that at any second my life is going to end.

I think of Devon. Of those last moments of his life. Were they like this? Suffocating on fear and silence and wonder until it was just over?

*No.*

"Get out of the car," Carlos tells me.

I open the door and hear the quiet in the empty lot next to the swimming hole. I expect Otis to come out of the woods, or maybe to see the headlights of his car. But I don't see anything. Carlos takes one of my hands and whips it around my back, then takes the other. Soon he's tying some kind of thick metal wire about my wrists. He does the same to my ankles. Then I hear a tearing sound. It's tape—thick, wide tape that he plasters over my mouth.

His hand pats the front of my pants and I jerk away from him until he curses and tells me to stand still. He finds my pocket and then shoves his hand in to grab my iPhone. I hear him toss it somewhere into the woods.

"If anyone comes looking for that, they'll find it right here," Carlos says.

He laughs. This is why he brought me here. I guess Carlos and Otis are no longer buddies.

I feel his hands guide me to the edge of the backseat and then shove me in.

*No.*

I remember what Harry said back in the record store.

*Go away, devil. Get out of here.*

The door shuts; then I hear him get in the front and start the car. We drive off.

My arms are already burning. I try to move my hands, but it's impossible. I feel the car turn, then stop, then turn, then drive. I have no idea where we might be headed.

*Get away, devil.*

"You know something, kid," Carlos says after moments of silence. "I gotta tell you—I give you credit. That whole thing you pulled back in Chicago. I didn't see that coming. Obviously."

I smell cologne. The guy is hiding from the police and he still has time to wear cologne. He has a slight Mexican accent that seems to come out more when he's talking normal and not threatening.

"Of course, that human wreck that bailed you out . . . I've been watching him too. I don't need to bother doing anything to him. He's not going to last much longer living like that anyway. How in the world he managed to rescue you—I don't know."

*Maybe it can happen again.*

Maybe Nick Hamilton will come out of the darkness with guns blazing. Or maybe some car will come crashing out of the blue into my Honda, just the way one did when my completely drunk father once took me out for a little terror ride.

"You know how easy it is to stay hidden? What a joke. It makes me think the authorities aren't too worried about a dumb Mexican they probably assume is south of the border by now. But I've been watching. I've been watching you and my pretty little niece."

The SUV slows down, then turns again. I don't hear anything outside, but I can't really hear anything except the engine and Carlos.

"People today—everybody's so busy. You let a month or two pass, and it doesn't matter what happens—people forget. The world moves on. But I don't forget, Brandon."

He curses in Spanish. Or maybe tells me what he's going to do to me.

I squirm again and try to move. Parts of my body are falling asleep and getting tingly.

*God, please be here please, God, help me.*

A weird feeling begins to spill inside me. Just like the burning ache flowing throughout. It's not fear. That's there of course, like concrete at the base of a house. But there's something more. Something that I've been getting more and more used to feeling.

*Fury.*

The sensation is a bit like what I felt when I finally confronted my father. When I went in and did something and didn't hold back. I can't do anything now, but I feel okay. Is this God watching out for me and giving me this sense of courage? I don't know. Maybe.

*Maybe God doesn't have to show up sitting in the backseat. Maybe he can fill me in some sort of way.*

Something inside me feels free. I don't know why, but it does, and I feel like I'm hovering over this place. I'm not bound and gagged and face-first in the backseat of my own car. All I know is that I'm still alive and this monster has me and he doesn't have Marvel and I'm glad for it because if I can and when I can I'm going to hurt him.

*You're an idiot.*

Maybe I am an idiot. But this is the same idiot who stood up to his stupid drunk of a father. Who stood up to those thick muscleheads beating up Seth. Who tried to stand up to the guy driving this car, who survived him once.

*I'll survive you again, you pig.*

I'm not sure if this kind of anger is good. What's that called? Righteous anger? No. This isn't that kind. Because if I could I'd hurt Uncle Carlos, I'd hurt him bad.

But this fury keeps me burning and breathing.

I can't do anything else. Just burn inside and breathe in and out.

*You can keep asking God to be here. Keep telling the devil no.*

I might die tonight, but I might kill too. I don't know. But Marvel isn't here, Marvel is safe, and that's a win. Because that's been my goal, my promise all along.

Perhaps, maybe, my end.

# 42

It's pitch black outside when I'm pulled out of the backseat. I'm drowsy, not just from being in the same position for such a long time (an hour, maybe longer?) but from the blood not moving through my system. The cool night air and Carlos's violent handling jerks me awake. My eyes try to focus on what's around me but there's nothing I can see. The sky isn't helping since it's overcast tonight.

Carlos holds me in place and cuts the wire with his knife. Then he shoves me forward. He pushes me through a door and into a hallway, then whips me around as I bang into a wall. I hear a door open as he orders me to go down the steps. I take them slowly since there's no light on.

A bulb overhead bursts on, and I squint and try to adjust. We're in a small, unfinished basement.

"Move to the back," Carlos says.

He takes me by a water heater and handcuffs me to it. There's nothing else down here. I can't help but think of an episode of *Breaking Bad*. Things didn't turn out so well for that guy.

*Let's hope Carlos hasn't seen that show.*

I expect him to tell me his plan or to curse in Spanish or say something, but he just leaves me alone. The light goes back off. My left hand is hanging off the pipe that I'm cuffed to. The cold slab I'm sitting on couldn't be more uncomfortable. I rip the tape off my mouth and suck in a breath.

For a while I just pray and keep praying. Begging God not only to hear me but to get me out of here. To rescue me. To make the dark go away. To do anything.

*Except bring Marvel here.*

I guess that it's not good to qualify your prayers. I can't help it. I don't want Marvel anywhere around here.

"*He told me I would be used for his power and his glory.*"

Her words feel as real as the moment she said them to me. The time she finally told me the truth about what happened in her old home with her father and the rest of her family and how God had spared her life.

"*I would be used in an awe-inspiring way.*"

*No, no, no,* I say over and over again. I didn't want to hear her words then and I don't want to remember them now.

"*He said my name . . .*"

I feel tears coming down my cheeks. Maybe because I'm scared for me or maybe for Marvel or maybe for both of us. Or maybe I'm feeling sorry for myself. Maybe I'm just tired.

"*I knew I was okay. I knew I was loved. I knew I was protected.*"

I know I have to believe like Marvel. This is what I'm supposed to do. This is what I *must* do.

So I ask to believe, to have that kind of assurance. But I don't.

*"I would be used in an incredible way."*

I don't want her used in any way, incredible or not. Not for me. Not for *this*. Please, God, no.

*"He said I would die being used in this way."*

More tears. The sinking, falling feeling.

Black smothering silence tucked away in the corner of a basement in nowhere. Unseen and unheard except by one.

*"There can be no Graham without Berry."*

My own silly, sappy words, bringing more tears. I brace myself to stop and be strong. Then I remember being in the cold water of Lake Michigan. Another black hole of despair. Crying out again. To one.

Hearing the one. Hearing him then, and once again hearing him now in my soul.

TRUST IN ME FOR I AM GOOD.

He heard and he saved me.

I'm safe now. I know this.

CALL ON MY NAME IN YOUR DISTRESS AND I WILL ANSWER YOU.

I wipe my face with my free hand and feel my head nodding an urgent yes even though there's no need. But it's for me. It's to show God. I'm going to trust. I'm going to call his name. I'm going to be terrified, how can I not be? But I'm going to give the terror over to him.

"No, devil, get out of here and stay away."

I grit my teeth and close my eyes.

So many things swirl inside my mind as I shift my body, trying to get a little comfortable. Marvel's voice again. Harry and my father and my mother and my brothers and Devon and so many others. A song I remember listening to with Marvel plays in my head.

*"Stay awake with me, take your hand and come and find me."*

I replay them in my head as my prayer. I pray that God doesn't go to bed somewhere up there in the skies. That there's no slumbering on his watch. I ask him to stay awake all night and bring his hand down from heaven and somehow allow me to be found.

Again.

# 43

I want to keep strong. To keep praying. To keep telling the devil to take a hike and to ask God to come down. But eventually I stop. Tired and scared and unsure, but mostly just tired.

I lose track of the time in the basement. I know it's gotta be the day after Carlos took me, but in the black I can't tell time. I just know I'm aching and thirsty and wondering if I'm going to die. At one point he comes back down and turns on a light and examines me without a word. He gives me a bottle of water and takes off, leaving the light on. I'm not sure if this is him having a little compassion or what.

Later that day (or maybe it's nighttime again) he comes back, walking strangely, as if he just woke up. When he gets closer I smell liquor. I've had quite a bit of experience detecting it. Maybe this isn't unusual for Carlos, or maybe he's drinking because he's got a guy chained to the water heater in the basement.

*This guy killed Devon; he doesn't care a bit.*

He stands over me, far enough away that I couldn't reach him even if I tried. There's something dead in his eyes. It's not just some kind of blank gaze; it's detached. Zombielike. The angry fire I saw when he was telling me to leave Marvel alone or that he was going to get me is gone. His eyes look empty, and because of that they also look terrifying.

"They're talking about you," Carlos says, shaking his head and laughing in a disgusted sort of way. "Boy, are they talking about you."

"Who?"

"Who do you think?" he says. "Everybody. Saw your mom."

"What? Where?"

I straighten up and feel the needles in my back and my butt.

"On the news. Crying her eyes out. 'Oh, my son. Please bring back my boy if you're watching this—'"

He curses and then spits on the floor. I wonder if he's just trying to look all mean and tough and bad guy–like.

"They don't get it. They just don't."

I remain silent. I'm pretty sure he's not going to listen to me or answer anything I ask.

He squats so he can face me square-on.

"There's a point in life when you realize there's no going back," Carlos says. "When you realize you're not even going to bother turning around. You know? Maybe you don't. But I still remember—I was younger than you—shooting someone for the first time. You know what I felt? I wasn't scared. I wasn't worried the guy I shot was going to die. He didn't. I really wished he had. This feeling—it was freedom. I felt like this thing was lifted off me. I suddenly realized that I could do anything I wanted."

I breathe in and can feel myself trembling as I breathe out.

"You want to know why I took you? I'm going to kill you and then show Marvel. It's not going to be dramatic, like bringing her your head in a box. That's too much work. But I want her to know. I made a promise to her. I told her once that I would kill you and I'd show her your corpse right before I killed her."

He clenches his jaw and grits his teeth, nodding to himself and looking around as if trying to figure things out.

I cough and wipe the sweat off my forehead. The hazy glow of the bulb above us seems to pulse like a heart that's slowing down and about to stop. I hear the jingle of my cuff against the iron pipe as I adjust my arm.

"Do you know anything about cancer, Brandon?"

I don't want to say anything to this psycho. Some might try to reason their way out of this, but I don't think there's a thing I can say that's going to stop what he's going to do, so I just listen.

"My mother had cancer. For years it ate away at her insides and nobody ever knew about it. By the time they discovered it, it was too late. She had only weeks to live. She died fast and furious. If only she'd known, right?"

He balls up his fists. There's nothing relaxed about Carlos right now. Even if he might be ready and happily willing to kill me any moment, I can tell he's not feeling overly confident about anything.

"You don't get it, but I do. There's a cancer in Appleton, and nobody sees it. Except a handful, of course. Your tall friend—he knew. He knew better than most. Otis Sykes wants me dead, just like you. When I'm done with Marvel and you, I'm going to kill him. But first things first."

The fact that he mentions Devon again angers me, and I break my silence.

"What does Otis want? What's this cancer you're talking about?"

His eyes seem to darken. "You wouldn't understand if I told you. Imagine a town being overrun by the enemy. Yet the people go on living life without a clue. And even after this all ends—you and me and Marvel—they'll just move on, because that's what people do."

I still don't understand. Carlos just curses and laughs.

"Otis used to call me a dumb wetback. I'm not dumb, Brandon. I've got stuff on him that will put him away. And freak out the world. Not little Appleton reporters talking to mothers, but the world, Brandon. *El mundo entero.*

"Some of the things that guy said—I think he's spent too much time by himself. Doing all that weird devil stuff. I just know he's a sick old man who has a lot of money. And he gave me a lot of it. But this didn't start in his sweet little town. It started next door."

I'm about to say something, then pause. When Carlos sees my expression, he still looks amused.

"Nobody knows," he says. "And nobody really cares. Not when it's some Mexican kid. And *especially* not when it's some poor black kid from the city. But a white suburban boy? Followed by a pretty white suburban girl?"

He curses in a furious, ugly way, as if he just spit a big loogie into my face.

"And everybody wants to point fingers at the scary spic. The mean-looking guy. Obviously I must have killed that stupid white kid from your school. Nobody's looking at the silly and stupid older perv who wallows around in his aloha shirts."

Hawaiian shirts? Does he mean Lee Fleisher, the friendly shopper at the record store? The guy who wanted me to snowblow his driveway?

*And yeah, that went not particularly well.*

"The guy named Lee—are you talking about him?"

Carlos shakes his head, not in a way that responds to my question but more like annoyed that I even asked it. He curses as he stands.

"I'm tired of watching everybody talking about another missing suburban teen and showing my picture. They're not going to find me. Not here. You ever hear of Earlville? A thousand people around here. Absolutely no connection to me whatsoever. A drug dealer from Chicago owned this place. Well, he still does, but he's in Lake Michigan decomposing, so yeah, I wouldn't say he vacations out to Earlville too often. It was his safety net. Now it's mine. I could hide here for a while or just take off, but there's one more thing I have to do first."

Another curse, another spit.

"You know—you want to know just how many times I wanted to show Marvel what I thought of her? Her and that long, tight body of hers?"

A sudden cold, clawing sensation fills me. Those dead eyes look at me without blinking.

He laughs, and I feel sick to my stomach.

"My wife—she kept me off of her. That woman is the only

soul on this planet to have any sort of say with me. But if I knew how all this would play out, I wouldn't have listened or waited. I would have stopped simply *watching*."

He heads over to the stairway, then stops.

"I'm done watching, kid."

The light goes out, and once again I'm left alone.

# 44

For some reason, in between nodding off or simply growing numb from the pain and the terror, I think of something Marvel wrote.

I remember her blog about Superman.

*It wasn't a blog—it was something she e-mailed you. You read it and told her she should start a blog.*

That's right.

I just remember it because it was pretty inspiring then. I try to remember it as best I can.

All I remember are the last words.

"*A Superman awaits. And not even Kryptonite will stop him.*"

I sigh.

Yeah.

# 45

Something rattles and shakes everything around me. It's late—very late, I assume but don't know—and my stupor is suddenly torn apart by an explosion.

*What . . . ?*

My eyes have to shut because the light everywhere is so bright. As the shaking stops, I bring both hands up to shield my face, and that's when I realize the one is no longer stuck in a cuff.

*This can't be happening. It's another one of those dreams.*

I brace myself, pushing off my heels and stretching to try to stand. I feel blood moving back into the places it had shifted away from. As I gain my focus, I'm able to see an outline in the light, a tall and massive figure looming over me.

*Come on, Brandon, wake up; you're seeing things.*

But I feel a grip and then see a face looking at me. It's not Carlos. It's someone I've never seen, yet he looks familiar.

"Hurry and get up," he tells me.

His voice is calm and quiet but urgent. I'm a bit shaky, but the man beside me helps me stand.

"Come on," he orders, pulling me through the basement. "Quickly."

The spotlight has faded, and now I'm seeing the afterglow in the dark. The man helps me up the stairs. "This way," he says in a voice barely above a whisper.

There's a small lamp on at the top of the stairs. He pulls me through the open doorway and down a hall. The front door of the house is wide open, and we walk through it and head outside.

The air and my breathing and the sweat covering me and the way my legs and my back prickle and the slight breeze against my skin all tell me this is not a dream.

The moon above glows, making me think of the blood moon the night before. The moon that I missed. My Honda Pilot is missing, but I see an old car sitting near us.

I look at the man who just brought me up here. He doesn't look like a cop or Navy SEAL or anybody official. He's wearing jeans and an ordinary jacket. He has an ordinary haircut. He's a guy you'd never really bother looking at 'cause he's just so ordinary.

*Am I dreaming? What were the shaking and the light?*

I can't help it. I stop and stare at the guy who rescued me.

"Brandon, don't stop. Keep running."

So I do, following him. I feel like my feet are my own again. And I no longer feel the stranger's grip on my arm.

We get on the road and start running. The farther from the house we go, the more I can see the stars above me. Wherever we are, it's far from the town and neighborhoods

I've known, where the sky doesn't look this bright. The universe feels like it's hovering inches from my face, ready to fall like ashes from a million fireworks.

As I jog, I glance back at the house we've just escaped from.

"Don't look back," the man tells me. "Don't ever look back at the darkness, Brandon."

I look toward him but suddenly I can't see anybody. My eyes are still adjusting from that flash.

*But it's not that dark and he just disappeared and what is happening.*

"Tell the world how you've been saved," the voice says.

And then I see something I can't understand, but which explains everything.

A brilliant light coats the trees and casts beams through the limbs and branches. Like some kind of fireball without the flames. Like a meteorite blasting without the debris. I slow down as I wince and shield my eyes and realize . . .

*You were just rescued by an angel.*

"Run," the voice says, now distant but still urgent. "Run down this road and don't stop. Stay away from any cars. Get to town and get help."

So I do as I'm told, still trying to figure out—

"The prayers of those who love you brought me here," he calls out. "Your heavenly Father interceded."

The voice and the light both vanish, and I know it's true. An angel came for me.

To rescue me.

Just as Marvel was rescued from the fire her father set.

She'd been in flames while I was in darkness. It didn't matter. Neither mattered, because both of us were set free.

*But why? Why me? Why?*

I keep running and panting and trying to breathe, and all the while I hear those words in my head.

"*Tell the world . . .*"

# 46

As soon as I see some houses, I think somehow I need to get a vehicle and then drive back to Aurora, back to Marvel. But I don't know how I could do this, and the only thing I really can do is tell the cops what happened. And before that I have to call Marvel.

My dirt road turns to a gravel road, and I'm running past fields instead of trees. Vast, dark fields. I pass a farm and see the silos sticking out like soldiers guarding the road. With my luck they're two seconds away from turning into towering demons that will try to squash me. I realize I'm still half-delirious because of the whole being-chained-up-in-a-basement thing.

*You're never gonna look at a water heater in the same way again.*

Lights ahead of me give me some hope. They're not the bright, shiny lights of the golden gates of heaven. At least I hope that's not what I'm seeing. I wonder if there will be fast-food restaurants in heaven. Why wouldn't there be? The food will no longer be bad for you, and you won't be in a rush in the first place. But those McDonald's fries are so good and they could be free and all-you-can-eat and you can just—

*Snap out of it. Be alert and stop thinking of food.*

I cross a bigger street but keep walking. Soon I'm passing houses, a neighborhood of sorts, but I keep walking to find some kind of store. I don't know if it's night or morning or the exact center point between the two, when everybody except deranged Mexican killers is awake. I find a grocery store but it's asleep as well. For a minute I wonder if I should wake somebody up, but I decide not to. That's how people get shot these days. Especially someone looking like I do. A sweaty, scared mess. I go to the back of the store and hide behind a Dumpster. The smell isn't very good, but at least I'm out of sight.

I hear a couple of cars drive by. Maybe one of them is Carlos. Who knows.

I lean against the metal bin and nod off till the sound of more vehicles wakes me up.

I hear a car turn in to the store parking lot and stop; then a door opens and shuts. I hold my breath. The glow of the lights turning on outside the store makes me breathe easily again. I stand up and look around the parking lot before heading over to the glass door. It's locked, but I can see a guy inside. He looks like a Harry-type of guy, older and nice and hopefully willing to help me out.

For a moment he checks me out, but then he walks over, apparently thinking I look harmless or maybe just figuring he could take me out if necessary (which is surely true).

"Store doesn't open till five," he says in a slight drawl.

"I need to call the cops."

I see wrinkles underneath eyes that look like they just woke up. He studies me.

"You okay, son?"

I let out a sigh and shake my head and try to be strong. Then I feel my face crinkle as I begin to sob.

"Hey, hey, what's going on—what's wrong?"

I've never done something like this before, but I wrap my arms around this stranger and cry an insanely joyful sort of cry.

After I tell him a jumbled, abbreviated story of what happened to me, showing him my wrist just to make sure he knows I'm not lying, the man grabs his cell and calls the police. He tells them I'm the boy on the news, the boy from Appleton who was missing.

Before he puts the cell phone away, I ask if I can borrow it. He doesn't hesitate or ask me why.

My hands shake as I try to dial Marvel's cell phone number. I have to stop and back up twice.

She picks up on the second ring. A hoarse, soft voice, pretty much the best sound I've ever heard in my life.

"Marvel, it's me," I say after her unsure greeting. "I'm okay. I'm here. I'm borrowing someone's cell. I'm okay."

"Brandon?" she says in a louder voice. "Is that really you?"

"Yes."

"What happened? Where are you?"

"I'm safe. The police are coming. I'm in some town. Carlos—he got me. But I'm okay, I swear I'm fine."

All I can hear are muffled sobs. I tell her again I'm fine and to listen.

"Marvel, look, do not leave your place. Call my mom and tell her I'm okay. I'm fine. Then call the cops and tell them, okay? Tell them I've been found. The police here are coming and I'll let them know about everything. I'm going to be fine. But you be careful. I don't know where Carlos is, but I know he wants to kill you."

She still can't talk.

"Marvel?"

"Yes." So faint and weak.

"Call the cops, okay? And be careful."

"How'd you get away?" she asks.

I feel goose bumps as I think about it again. "I'll tell you later. God took care of me. Okay? Call the cops and then stay put. I'll get there as soon as I can. Okay?"

"I love you, Brandon."

"I love you too."

If she only had a clue of how much. If she only realized how insufficient those three words happen to be.

Then again, hearing her say them is enough. I wasn't sure I'd ever hear them from her or anyone again.

# 47

An hour later I lose my mind in the front seat of an unmarked police car. The cop at the wheel literally has to pull over and grab my wrist to stop my pounding on the dashboard.

"She's fine, they're fine," he tells me.

But for a moment I'm not listening. I'm just yelling at him to drive, to get to Marvel, to get there faster. I don't care if he says she's fine. I don't believe it.

"Listen to me, Brandon: Carlos is dead. Do you understand? He showed up, and the police chased him, and he ran in front of a truck. Brandon, chill. Stop freaking out. Your girlfriend is fine. She's alive. The officer I just spoke to is with her."

Even though I have some liquid and food and pain medication inside my stomach, I still feel completely cracked open, like an egg with the yolk spilling out. That's my brain, and it's leaking onto this seat and onto the cop beside me.

Once he starts driving again, going at least thirty miles over the speed limit on this small highway, I calm down enough to ask him to tell me exactly what happened.

And as he does, I feel a sense of déjà vu.

*I dreamt about this.*

I know exactly what he's saying because it was in one of those crazy nightmares I had months ago, before I found Carlos and Otis meeting up at the warehouse—the one I went inside to check out, the one I almost got caught snooping around in.

*But I thought Carlos was chasing me in the dream?*

The cop said Carlos drove close to the cousin's apartment where Marvel is staying. He parked the car and started walking on foot. A cop spotted him and began chasing.

I see Carlos smiling, his face splattered with blood.

"Moron got run over by a truck. Didn't live much longer. It was pretty ugly, I hear."

I remember this scene. Carlos all mangled up on the street.

*Wasn't there a sword somewhere in the picture?*

I shut my eyes and see him coughing up blood, choking on it.

"They said the guy was laughing when he died," the cop tells me.

Once again, a dream I had ended up happening. But how? Or maybe I should ask why? In what way was I involved? Did I have any impact on it happening?

I hear Carlos's words in my dream.

*"You have no idea what kind of monster's been unleashed. This is only the beginning. I'm just surveying the land before the troops arrive."*

Did he say this to somebody before he died? I don't know.

With our car heading east toward the rising sun, I feel a blast of hope just like the radiance in front of me.

*This is what was going to happen. This was the thing Marvel needed to do. This is how she helped save others.*

With Uncle Carlos coming back for her. With my help too. With the kidnapping and all.

*"He said I'd save others from something."*

That's what Marvel did tonight. Or this morning.

*"He said I would die being used in this way."*

But maybe God changed his mind for some reason. He can do anything, right? He sent someone ordinary-looking but shining bright to save me.

*God, I hope this is what Marvel's been talking about all along. You spared her life, right? Right?*

# 48

When I finally reach Marvel, I grab her and hold her and tell her it's all right and tell her I never want to let her go.

# 49

In the end, my abduction leads to Uncle Carlos dying and Marvel finally being set free. That early morning is a circus of cops and reporters and family and friends. One moment that stands out in the midst of Marvel and me hovering in the center of this hurricane is her aunt coming over to give me a big hug and kiss. She says something in Spanish that sounds pretty complimentary. It's the most attention I've ever received from the woman. I'm guessing that she's pretty happy about everything.

Throughout the day—going to the police station, talking to several different detectives, having Mom and my brothers around me—Marvel stays by my side. At one point, as we're sitting alone in the family room in her cousin's apartment, waiting on another cop to talk with us, I ask Marvel how she's doing. How she's feeling and what she's really thinking about everything.

*If she's thinking what I'm thinking.*
"I don't know," she says.

Her eyes still look puffy from all the tears, both happy and sad. She looks exhausted. I can't even begin to imagine what I look like. Thankfully I haven't passed any mirrors this morning to find out.

"I know what you're thinking," she says.

"What?"

She glances around to see if anybody can hear us talking. "I don't know if this changes anything."

"How could it not?"

She shrugs. "Maybe it does. I'm hoping. But I don't know."

"Do you feel any different? Or have you seen or heard—?"

"No."

I've waited this long to tell her, but I can't wait any longer.

"Marvel—it was an angel," I whisper. "An angel, seriously. Like, the bright lights kind. It saved me."

She looks up, serious and focused and waiting for more.

"He told me that the prayers of others had been heard. He also told me to share this, to tell others about being rescued."

Some kind of shift occurs as I feel her clutch my hand. "What did he look like?"

"Normal," I say. "Like totally just some regular guy. But he appeared in a blinding light—disappeared that way too. My handcuffs were off."

"You told the police you woke up and found them off."

"I did," I said. "But what? I'm not telling them an angel rescued me. I mean—they'll think I'm crazy."

The tears popped up again in her eyes.

"What?" I ask.

"Maybe you're right," she says in a barely audible voice.

"I couldn't stop praying. I couldn't stop asking God why. To help you. To take me."

"Stop."

"I did. You're not a part of this, Brandon. You weren't in that closet when I heard God talking to me."

"I am now. I found you, and I'm stuck in the closet with you. Like it or not."

She wipes her cheeks and grips my hand again. "Maybe we'll be okay. Maybe."

"*We* are going to get married in just a couple weeks and we are going to have that happily ever after, Marvel. God saved me tonight. I think he heard you and decided to act. Carlos came after you, and you ended up helping a lot of people."

"But I didn't do anything."

"So praying isn't anything?" I ask.

She looks at me and nods. She knows I'm right. I mean— how can't I be right? How can I know all this? Marvel's really changed me.

Maybe God's starting to change me too.

# 50

I'm finally back in my bed in a quiet house. Dad came around tonight. Mom allowed him to come and see me because of everything that happened, and the police didn't do anything since nobody was pressing charges and he could prove he was getting treatment. I didn't mind. Nothing big or dramatic happened. There were no special moments, no shared smiles, no strange conversations or sudden feelings of worry. It was very uneventful, which meant it was pretty much perfect.

It takes me a while to fall asleep. Soon I realize that maybe I should have waited just a bit longer to enter slumberland.

My dreams . . . they've been waiting for me. Like some kind of angry ex-girlfriend who shows up on your lawn with eggs. No, make that with a gun.

I'm sitting next to Marvel somewhere—I can't tell where—but I hear her start to scream. I try to console her and ask what's wrong and try to calm her, but she just pushes me away. Her face suddenly becomes twisted and furious as she stands and holds out her hands.

"It's time," she shouts.

All around us are screams, and I look to see where they're coming from but there's only smoke and fire.

"The energy of the D'Bari star will give me strength. The supernova will make me a god."

Marvel looks down at me with wide eyes, blood leaking from them like crimson tears, and her voice becomes low and awful sounding.

"I will have my vengeance," she shouts.

There's an explosion and gunfire and more screams, and I try to grab her but I can't. I keep reaching but I can't do anything. Then I realize why.

My hand is cuffed to the chair next to me.

And the laughter begins while screams and smoke start to devour me . . .

Then I finally wake up.

I turn on the light in my room and just sit for a moment, happy to be back here, safe. I try to process what just happened.

*I dreamt about Carlos dying and he did, so does that mean this is going to happen?*

But I tell myself I've dreamt of other things, too. Other things that didn't happen.

The dreams. The visions. The angels. The nightmares. I think this is seriously how a person loses his mind. Maybe I've already lost mine.

I write down on a sheet of paper what I heard Marvel—or whoever that was that looked like her—said.

*D'Bari star supernova*

I'm too tired to open my computer and search for it, but I tell myself I'll do it tomorrow. Whenever tomorrow comes.

# 51

When I get to school, every single person greets me with a hello or a cheer or a clap or a handshake. I even get a few hugs. Frankie and Barton walk into the building with me and take it all in.

"You always wanted to be the star quarterback, right?" Frankie asks.

"I'll still never be as good-looking as you," I tell him.

Everybody knows what happened, of course. Even the teachers in the hallway are telling me how glad they are to see me.

Marvel isn't coming to school today. She's with her family, dealing with family stuff. It's not like there will be a funeral for Carlos, but they're still getting together—the small family who are in any way connected to Marvel's aunt. I'm planning to head over to their house after school. For the family wake, hallelujah-Carlos-is-dead celebration.

I feel guilty for the thought. *Respect the dead, idiot.* It's going to take a while to let go of Carlos and what he did. To all of us.

Before my first class someone comes up behind me.

"You made it," Seth says.

Standing there out of breath, with an almost fully shaved head and beady eyes, he looks strung out or something.

"Are you okay?" I ask him.

He shakes his head in a *no* way but then says yes.

He's wearing a Joy Division T-shirt with black cargo pants.

"What's going on?" I ask him.

"I thought you died."

His face looks scared and wounded, more than ever before.

"I didn't."

Seth looks around and nods, then tries to compose himself.

"Do you know 'It's only after we've lost everything that we're free to do anything'? A quote from *Fight Club*."

"Yeah," I say. "Well, I didn't lose everything."

"I thought I did," Seth says.

He looks like he wants to say more but he doesn't. I watch him dart away in an awkward sort of walk.

Before lunch I text Marvel to see how she's doing. She's fine and misses me and wishes I were with her. I don't tell her about the welcome I received today. I'll tell her later when I see her.

I'm sitting with Frankie and Barton when I hear the news.

"Did you hear? Greg Packard got expelled."

I look at Frankie in total disbelief. "When?"

"Yesterday. Seth finally went to the principal. And to the police. As if they didn't have enough to deal with."

"Are you serious?"

"I bet Greg's father chained him up to a water heater," Barton says.

Frankie hits him. "Not cool, man."

"It's fine," I say. "What else can I do but laugh? I just can't believe Seth did it."

"Yeah," Barton says, mouth full of Doritos. "Could he be any more of an outcast?"

"Maybe if people like *you* tried a little harder to be friendly, he wouldn't be."

"Principal and cops ended up talking to me to validate his story," Frankie says. "I'm wondering if they'll talk to you."

"They're probably tired of talking to me. What with Devon and my father and now Carlos."

"You're like a walking disaster movie," Barton says.

I just look at Frankie and shake my head. Even if I'm suddenly homecoming king and star quarterback mixed into one, Barton is still going to give me crap.

"It's nice to have the support," I joke.

"Did they ever find your car?" Frankie asks.

"Nope. I'm thinking with my luck, I shouldn't have either. 'Cause crazy people tend to ruin them." I look at Barton, who doesn't miss my reference to my first car, which he drove into a pit another lifetime ago.

"Is that a way to ask for your money?" he says.

"What? You still owe me money?"

I honestly don't know. When I see his look—guilt and humor and stupidity—I realize that yes, he definitely still owes me money.

"You're unbelievable," I say.

"I'll get it to you this summer."

"Uh-huh. Why don't you just include it in your wedding present to Marvel and me?"

"We're supposed to get you a present?" Barton asks.

He's serious, too.

"You're just plain dumb," Frankie tells him.

I laugh. It's good to see these guys. Even if the fourth chair at the table is empty.

# 52

I'm walking out of a Walgreens when I see him. It goes through my head that this definitely isn't some kind of cool action movie. I'm certainly not the right hero, and a scene like this would never be set in front of everybody's favorite pharmacy. But Mom asked me to pick up her prescription and I need some deodorant and hey there's the evil villain waiting outside for me.

I see the black Lincoln parked across the lot from the entrance, and even though I can't see inside it, I know who's sitting in the driver's seat. I pause and feel the nice fifty-degree afternoon breeze. I'm not sure how long I stand there, but I don't back down or head the other way.

I decide to walk over to the car. Toward Otis Sykes, whom I'm supposed to stay away from. Whom I'm legally required to stay away from.

As I approach the car, I see the window sliding down. The old sinister face stares at me with no emotion.

"What do you want?" I ask.

He laughs. "This isn't doing a very good job of keeping away from me, is it?"

His voice is slow and relaxed, but very careful sounding as well. His round, bald head makes him look old, but not for a minute do I think this man is weak. I'm fueled by anger that overcomes the fear in the pit of my stomach.

"Why are you spying on me?" I ask. "Harassing me."

"The mystery is over, Brandon. Do you understand? The cops got the bad guy. The killer is in the afterlife now. There's no need for you to be Watson anymore. Your Sherlock Holmes is already dead."

I can't help the curse that comes out of my mouth, but all it does is make Otis laugh more.

"Ah, so many things you don't understand. That feeling inside of you—that hate and energy and belief that you can *change* things? Be the hero? I admire it. But you don't understand, Brandon. Nothing is going to change here. You can't do a thing. Look what happened to Devon. Look at Carlos. Look at your pitiful father."

Devon died a hero and Carlos got caught and my father is trying to change.

*There are things you don't understand either.*

"They're going to find out one day," I tell him. "I promise."

He shakes his head and sighs. "So naive, young man. So foolish."

The expression on his face suddenly turns dark and scary. His eyes become slits like razor blades and I can see his teeth bared, like a snarling dog.

"Brandon—you're a smart kid, right?"

"Yeah."

"Good. So stay smart. And if you want to stay alive, stay away."

"From what?" I ask.

"From me. From all of this."

He rolls up his window and then pulls out of the parking spot. I watch the car disappear into the rest of the afternoon traffic.

I stand there in the parking lot and look up to the heavens.

"God, help me let others know about this evil man. Help me do whatever I can to take him down. Send someone to help me. Help me, please."

I know my prayer is heard. I don't know what will happen.

But I know something. I promise—I vow right here and now—that I'm not going to back down and I'm not going to stay away from Otis.

He's the reason behind all of these bad things, I know it. I know it without a shred of doubt.

# 53

It's Thursday, April 18. A week and a half ago I was almost a dead man. In two days I'm going to legally get married and the next day, on Easter, Marvel and I will be officially married in front of a small group of people at my house.

All of that, and yet I still have to be sitting in English class listening to a discussion about a novel called *The Stranger* that I didn't read. I would read a five-hundred-page book on poetry if it was written by Marvel, but novels just aren't my thing. I really have no idea what the class is talking about. My teacher has mercy on me and doesn't call on me like she used to at the beginning of the year.

Hey, I'm the local town hero. I don't have time to read novels when I'm chained to a water heater or escaping from the bad guy. And honestly—when people read quotes like "Since we're all going to die, it's obvious that when and how don't matter," it doesn't really sound like the feel-good sort of story I need about now. It sounds more like a novel Seth wrote.

The whole wedding thing. It's crazy. Honestly. When I'm just sitting here and seeing the other room full of bored students, some listening and some daydreaming like me, it seems surreal that in a classroom not far away sits the love of my life. She's so close. I could just get up and run out of here and grab her hand and take her away. We could drive down south.

*You don't have a car.*

That's right. Also, I don't have that much money, having spent everything I had on the wedding. There's the money Seth owes me, but I don't know when I'll get that back.

"The symbolism is striking with such simple language . . . ," the teacher says.

*Blah blah blah.*

When is the bell going to ring? When can I get out of here and see that smile again? It's almost lunch. I'll be working one last time before the weekend. Lots to do. Then again, there's really only one thing to do.

*To say I do.*

I glance over and see Barton dozing in his seat. Nothing symbolic there. He's just plain bored and nearly unconscious.

I'd never want to be a high school teacher.

A little later, as I'm heading over to find Marvel before lunchtime, Seth pops out of nowhere and stops me.

"Hey, Brandon. I got a favor to ask."

I shake my head. "I don't have any more money."

"No, no. It's not that."

A couple of people bump into him as they're walking. They don't bump into me even though I'm standing right there too. But that's what it's like for Seth, especially after

Greg's expulsion. He's the school pariah. We move over to let the flow of traffic by.

"It's about Jeremy," he says.

I just groan. "Why don't you just leave that guy alone?"

"He's not leaving *me* alone. That's the thing."

"You still owe him money."

Seth looks around, then nods. He appears guilty and nervous.

"What's wrong? What's going on with him?" I ask.

"I have one thing to ask you. One more favor. That's all."

"What is it?"

"He wants me to meet him tomorrow, just after lunch. I told him I could slip out of school then. We have another one of those bullying sessions in the theater and I'd rather not spend an hour being looked at and pitied. I don't need to hear that lecture. I could give the thing myself."

I think of Jeremy, with his muscles and veins and tattoos.

"What's he want you to do?" I ask.

"I don't know. I mean—I think he's going to give me some stuff to sell."

Seth doesn't say what that "stuff" happens to be, but I'm pretty sure I know. At least I know the general category.

"So what do you need me to do?"

He stumbles over his words, not sure of them, mumbling. I tell him to make sense.

"Look—I'm just scared. You know him."

"I know to stay away from him," I say.

"It's too late for that. I owe him. It's just—he wants to meet at the quarry, and I want someone to be there. Looking out for me. In case—just in case. You know?"

I sigh.

*Yeah, just in case.*

I picture Devon saying these words. In fact, I sorta remember us having a similar conversation.

*Didn't you tell Devon to stop being stupid and leave it alone?*

Maybe if I could go back . . . Maybe if I could have stuck around and been more of a friend.

"I'll do it," I say.

"It's the last time, Brandon. Seriously."

Seth gives me an earnest and honest look, and I know he's telling me the truth.

"What time?"

"Can you get to the quarry by one?" he asks. "I'm skipping school, so I'll be coming from home. You can slip out at lunchtime."

"If I get in trouble I'm blaming you," I joke.

"If I get in trouble I'm blaming you."

I look at him and can tell he's not joking.

There's not much to do at the record store, and as usual there aren't any customers. But Harry's around, and eventually I ask him a question that's been on my mind.

"I was wondering something," I say. "About God."

He nods and looks a little surprised. "Well, I can try to answer it, but I'm no biblical scholar."

"I'm just wondering—does God ever change his mind? I mean—in the Bible. Are there examples of his saying something and then changing his mind?"

Harry puts down the stack of credit card slips in his hand and thinks for a minute. There's gothic eighties music playing in the background, which suddenly strikes me as funny. "Well . . . there's a time when God was going to punish the Israelites for their disobedience, but Moses begged him not to, and he didn't."

I nod. "So you think we have to be a Moses in order to get God to listen to us?"

He laughs. "You take a good look at Moses and you'll see someone with a lot of self-doubt. Someone with a real anger issue, too. I think the Bible tells us about warts and all to show that God uses ordinary, messed-up people to do his work."

I raise my eyebrows as if to say, wow, but really, I'm not sure what to think of this.

"My thought?" Harry says. "I think God's looking out for you. I think he's listening, too. A lot has happened since last summer. Don't stop talking to God, asking him for things. I know I haven't."

"Yeah."

As if on cue the bell rings, and we have a customer. I see the girl the moment she walks into the store.

*Déjà vu.*

"You guys hard at work or hardly working?" Marvel says, then quickly adds, "I just made that expression up, in case you're wondering."

"Hello, Miss Marvella," Harry says, going over and giving her a hug. "Are you still scheduled to work this weekend?"

Marvel laughs. "Well, I think that can happen. I might have to cancel a thing or two, but nothing too important."

"Ouch," I joke as she comes over and puts her arm around me. Not to hug but more to lock in.

"We were just having a deep conversation," I tell her.

"Let me guess—about eighties music?"

"A little deeper," Harry says. "But there's still time to have that conversation."

"Please, no," I say.

For a while it seems like old times, and I find myself thinking again just how awesome last summer was. When I couldn't wait to fill hours of my day next to this girl. It seems now like it was many years ago, simply because so many things have happened since. Both good and bad things.

"Are you guys going on a date?" Harry asks.

"Not a date," Marvel tells him. "Just hanging out. We're saving money."

"Well, I'm not sure I can let Brandon go. It's a busy night around here."

"We could close the store for you," she says.

Harry looks at her the way he'd glance at a daughter if he had one. "See, this is why I love you."

It's pretty hard *not* to love this girl.

# 54

The night seems to be holding its breath, listening to us. The river calls, this always moving, always playing body of water nearby. Neither of us has to say a word, and I think this is when I realize what love happens to be. Speaking without saying a word. Knowing without the need to ask. Letting the moments simply be.

We end up on the walkway beside the water and wander over to a small bridge that leads to a tiny island in the middle of the flowing water. In the middle of the bridge we stop.

"It's a beautiful night," Marvel says.

I stare at her and agree.

"Why are you smiling like that?" she asks.

"You know why."

"Uh-oh. Passionate Brandon Jeffrey. Watch out."

"Elope with me."

"I thought we were getting married pretty soon. In a matter of days—no, make that hours."

"Pretty soon doesn't sound soon enough."

"It will be worth the wait," she tells me.

It feels like the moon is reflecting Marvel's glow and not the other way around. This beam and this grinning burst of hope. I love this girl. So much. And I believe that it will be worth the wait to finally show and feel and give her all that's burning inside me.

"You're cute when you get like this," Marvel says.

"Do I look that desperate?"

She shakes her head, then moves closer and slides her arms around me. "You look safe. You look like a bridge on the edge of some burning town, leading to security."

"Safe, huh?" I ask her. My head is leaning down toward her, my nose touching her skin. "Some guys would prefer the girl says sexy."

"Sexy is like lighting a firework. It blows up and looks spectacular, but then it's gone. Security lasts forever."

"Then I'm very, *very* content to be your bridge, Marvel."

We kiss. And more than any way to describe it or paint the picture or sum up the fireworks inside of me at this moment, the best thing to say is that she simply fits with me. Her lips, her shadow, her glow, her story. A right hand with a left hand. Connecting and not letting go.

"Brandon?"

"Yes, Marvel," I say, stressing her name the way she stressed mine.

"I love you."

"I love you too."

"Don't forget."

"I don't plan to," I tell her, pulling her closer and then reminding myself with another kiss.

Kissing her will never get old. I just hope the two of us will always be side by side. Fitting just as well in old age as we do now.

# 55

The next day I wake up thinking about wedding plans and then spend most of the morning at school talking to Marvel and the guys about details. It's Friday, so a lot of students are already mentally checked out. I almost forget about meeting Seth until I get a text during break.

**You still coming? Quarry at one?**

*Oh yeah.*

I get that nervous feeling again. I think about the cemetery and the dogs in the field and wonder what might be next for Seth. Since this involves meeting Jeremy, my uneasiness is doubled. The way the guy drugged me at the Nine Inch Nails concert. Then the way he basically threatened me when he was looking for Seth.

*That's why Seth wants you around. Just in case.*

I think I've had a few too many just-in-cases recently. I really don't want another one.

**Yeah I'll be there.**

I haven't told Marvel, since I don't want her to either worry or give me a hard time about skipping school. But I decide I'd better, just in case someone decides to kidnap me and chain me to a water heater. I talk to her right before fourth period.

"Hey—I have to go somewhere at lunch. I won't be here to learn about bullying."

She looks genuinely disappointed. "Who am I going to sit with?"

I remember last fall when Marvel arrived, always on the outside, with her different outfits and attitudes. Now she has a bunch of girls who'd call her friend. Not Taryn's crowd, of course. They don't know what to do with a girl who looks like she's from the seventies, with her flowing dress and wedge heels and colorful vest.

"You get to sit with whoever. I'm sure you'll do fine. Just—text me to let me know anything I'm missing."

Marvel looks at me with suspicion. "Yeah, I'm sure you really want me to take notes. Where are you going? Is it a surprise?"

I could tell her yes, but I don't want to lie to her. There's no need.

"It's Seth."

"What about him?"

I glance around as I lower my voice. "He's meeting someone, and he wants me to be there and look out for him."

"Brandon."

"What?"

Now she looks worried. "Who is he meeting?"

"That guy I told you about—the fight club dude. You know, the crazy one?"

"Why is he meeting him?"

"I think he's in trouble," I say. "He just wants to make sure nothing crazy happens."

"Seriously," she says.

"No, come on. Listen, it'll be fine. Okay?"

"Are you meeting *with* them?"

I shake my head and smile to make sure she knows this is no big deal. "No, just watching from afar, I guess. It's fine. Seth skipped school today, so I'm just meeting him there. At the quarry."

"Brandon—"

"No big deal, okay? It'll give me time to think about my wedding vows."

"You still haven't thought of them?"

*Good. She doesn't look as stressed anymore.*

"I've thought about them. I just have lots of thoughts. Can't I just Google some good speeches and share that?"

"Tell me you're joking," she says.

"I'm joking."

"Okay—well, let me know what happens. I'll keep my phone on. I doubt they'll see me using it in the auditorium."

"Day's almost half over," I say and then kiss her on the cheek like a husband giving his wife a peck before heading off to work.

As always, Marvel seems to read my mind.

"Have a good day at work, *honey.*"

"Will do, my marvelous wife."

She walks off and I can't help watching, still stunned by her beauty, still surprised she somehow fell for me. I simply cannot wait for this weekend.

I'm a couple of blocks away from school, driving Frankie's car, and I'm stuck at a light when a concrete truck pulls up beside me. I glance over at the massive, towering thing in the left turn lane. The mixing drum is rolling around, and suddenly I think of Devon. I feel a wave of anger and sadness and hurt all mixed into one.

*Mixed into one good clever guy.*

But nothing about me is trying to be clever. I see a hose sticking out of the back of the truck and water slowly dripping out. I focus on the few little drops coming out. Then the truck turns and I'm brought back to reality.

*You don't want to end up in one of those, do you?*

I don't want Seth to, either. That's why I'm heading over to his house early to try to talk to him before he goes to the quarry. To either ride together or maybe persuade him not to go. Something's not right about the quarry. That's what Devon told me, and I still believe it. Otis lives there.

*There's a cancer in this place.*

The sun is bright and the sky blue, and it's just past noon when I get to Seth's. I park by the curb a house away from his and wait for about fifteen minutes, but I don't see anything. Just a nice house with a neatly cut lawn. I fumble with my phone and then open my backpack to look for my earbuds. I spot a black CD holder and realize it's the mix disc that Seth made me. I've never listened to it, partly because I forgot about it and partly because I haven't been in the mood for what I'm assuming is pretty wild and angry music. But I'm waiting for Seth himself, so I slip it in to see what it's like.

It begins with a muffled drumbeat and then wailing guitars playing a very moody tune. The singer blares out, "It doesn't matter if we all die." I sigh and laugh and select the next track. This one is all heavy metal, which I instantly change. Another violent track follows, another, then another.

*Not quite the inspiring CD that Harry gave me for my date with Marvel.*

I'm about ready to turn off the song when I hear one that's more electronic. It's by Nine Inch Nails, and I remember Seth telling me he loves this song. It's angry, talking about screaming and lashing out. Of course.

I'm waiting—it's maybe twenty till one—and I still don't see Seth.

The singer screams about burning the whole world down. I turn off the CD and look out my window, then look at my phone.

Nothing.

*Is he already there?*

I go ahead and text him.

**You coming?** I ask.

His reply comes quickly.

**I'm still at home leaving right now.**

But there's nothing happening at his house. No front door opening or garage door going up.

A sickening sort of feeling hovers over me. I decide to get out and go see if he's inside. Maybe just knock on the door to make sure.

Knocking gets me nothing. I blink and suddenly see an open door and a stairway heading up. Not like an image in memory but like some kind of burning billboard in my head.

A part of me fears going inside, fears being here in the first place. But something else, something deeper, urges me to go in.

Another text comes. **Will be there soon.**

*Is he still inside?*

I try the door. Unlocked, like always. Nobody is inside. Sunlight streams in from the windows.

"Seth?"

Nothing. I call his name a few more times. Look in the kitchen and family room. I blink and see the stairs again and they seem to be shivering. I feel my body trembling a little. I shake it off, knowing I shouldn't be nervous.

I go toward the front door and then decide to text Marvel.

**Hey—let me know if you see Seth okay? I can't find him.**

I wait a minute but don't get a reply. I slip my phone into my pocket and then head upstairs. Halfway up I see the closed door to his room.

*Maybe he's smoking some weed.*

I still don't hear or see anything. His door opens and I see a clean room, just like before. The bed is made; his desk is neat and orderly with the laptop on it.

I feel a buzz from my phone and see a message from Marvel.

**I'll look for him.** ☺

I'm about ready to leave—it's almost one—but I see a Post-it note on his laptop.

*You might want to check this out,* it says.

It's almost like the note is for me, but of course he doesn't know I'm here. Maybe he left himself a note for some reason. I look at the computer for a moment and hesitate, feeling like I'm already invading enough of his life. What would he say if he saw me opening his laptop?

*Check this out.*

I don't think the note is for Seth.

So I open the laptop.

A document is open and I peer down to read the text. It's some kind of manuscript—no, a PDF—and at the top of the page is this:

Battle not with monsters, lest ye become a monster, and if you gaze into the abyss, the abyss gazes also into you.

It's just more crazy, angry, weird Seth thinking. I scroll to the next page. There's a handwritten note that's shown in photo form. I can tell Seth wrote it.

*Dear World:*

*If you're reading this, that means it's done and I've won. I've destroyed the enemy and people will finally pay attention. They will know that hate can be fed and nurtured and that it can breed a Dark Phoenix that can destroy an alien race like the D'Bari and their solar system.*

*"The enemy has only images and illusions behind which he hides his true motives. Destroy the image and you will break the enemy."—ENTER THE DRAGON.*

*Today I will be destroying the image. Nobody will be able to hide. Today, the enemy will be exposed and ripped apart and eliminated.*

I'm shaking and can feel my heart pounding and I suddenly realize that something really, really wrong is happening here. I keep reading but I'm scanning now, looking ahead, wanting to hurry because this is *not good*.

> *This fifty-page report is called THE DARK PHOENIX MANIFESTO and inside it will list every little wrong inflicted upon me since I was ten years old.*
> *My plan . . .*
> *Carefully executed . . .*
> *The people who have hurt and tortured . . .*

I'm shaking my head and saying, "No no no no" and swallowing while I keep looking ahead.

> *Appleton High School will pay. Today.*

That's all I need to see. I blink and think of Seth being beaten up, being bullied and spotlighted to mock. The kamikaze headband . . . The Nietzche quotes about the meaninglessness of everything . . . The weird thing with Jeremy and the fight club and that video he said was made up showing him beating up people . . .

I grab my phone and don't see any messages.

*"I hate them all,"* I remember Seth saying.

My hand is shaking.

*The money he borrowed. From you.*

My breath feels buried and my throat thick and my heart is suddenly suffocating.

*The school assembly in the fine arts theater.*

My whole body is shaking when I make the call.

Maybe I should call the cops first, but I call Marvel. The phone rings and rings and rings and then I get her voice mail.

"Marvel, go to a teacher and tell them—something is happening, something with Seth—I don't know but I think—he's planning something. Tell the school. Tell somebody and get out of there. Tell somebody to lock the school down. I'm calling the cops. Please do it—"

I shut off the phone. I'm already bolting down the stairs and out the door and back to Frankie's car. I dial 911 as I start the car and begin racing toward the school. I tell them—I scream into the phone—the same thing I said to Marvel. I'm shouting and they're telling me to calm down and all I can say is that I believe something is about to happen at Appleton High and it might involve a student named Seth Belcher and my name is Brandon Jeffrey and on and on.

They tell me to stay on the phone but I shut off the call to see if Marvel called. There's no sign, no message, nothing. So I call her again and get her voice mail.

I speed down the side street and blow the stop sign and whip around the corner, hitting the curb and then building speed.

I can't stop the tears from falling down my face because I know. I just know.

# 56

Everything stops for a second.

    This breath choking in my throat seems to barricade the reality all around. Memories become my oxygen and I gasp them down.

    Marvella Garcia.

    The door opening and seeing her and feeling lighter.

    Talking with her the first time and seeing that smile.

    Trying and trying again and then trying a little more.

    The first time she confided in me. The first time I saw her cry. The first time I felt like I was her friend. The first time I somehow submerged into love.

    *You don't force love; it finds you.*

    And knowing this breaks me. Knowing this leaves me stranded now.

    I can't find my breath because I can't find a doorway to follow her inside. I can no longer chase after Marvel. I can no longer try, because Marvel is no longer.

    "God, no," my mouth and breath and life choke out.

That sound—my voice crackling out—brings me back to this race to the school. It's the longest drive of my life. I never knew that a place could be so far away, that a human could feel so remote, that time could shred itself so easily. I try calling Marvel over and over. I shake, yell, curse, pray, and I cry. My cheeks are lined with tears because I know.

I know now.

I know better and I know.

This is what it's all been leading up to and I know the outcome and yet I still drive hoping. I still drive wanting. I still drive expecting a different outcome and praying and gasping for air.

"Please, God—hear me—spare her—please."

I wipe my eyes, my face a sopping mess, while I drive through red lights and stop signs and street corners and slow-moving pedestrians.

But it's all for nothing.

Each blink is one where I see her.

Smiling.

Laughing.

Nudging.

Kissing my cheek.

Holding my hand.

Loving my broken and battered soul.

No.

Waving good-bye.

*No no no*

Telling me good-bye as she has over and over and over again.

"You saved me," I scream. "Save her. Save her. Save her like you saved me."

But I remember something as I turn down Main Street toward the high school. Toward the end.

*"I watched from the closet but I was protected. I was safe. Not a single hair on my head was singed."*

Marvel had already been saved. For this day. For this moment.

*No.*

I know that maybe things can be different. I believe it can be. God knows the story—he knows our plans—he knows this weekend we will be promising before *him* our lives and our future and maybe . . .

*"He told me I would be used for his power and his glory. That I would be used in an awe-inspiring way."*

Every *maybe* in my mind will never overcome the chorus of *no*s inside my soul.

I know.

When I finally glimpse the parking lot of Appleton High School, I see a swarm of cop cars and students flooding out behind them.

Life becomes a blistering fast blur. I race down one of the lanes even while students stream past me. I stop the car close to the entrance and see police guarding the doors and teachers guiding the students out.

*What did you do, Seth? What did you do?*

I'm going the wrong way and I feel hands grabbing at me and voices calling out but I break past and run toward the fine arts theater.

Someone grabs me and holds me down and I'm crying and screaming but it's not enough. Voices yelling and ordering me and asking me questions and shouting out to others.

I look out through the blur at other students crying like I am. Desperate. Angry. Scared.

And then I hear someone say the thing I never wanted to hear.

"She stopped him."

I'm being held back by a couple of cops and I feel the sky above me opening up.

I know Marvel is dead.

I know this is how the story ends because she always knew it would end this way. From the very beginning, I'd lost her.

From the very beginning, she was never mine to have.

I close my eyes and just say the same word over and over again.

"No."

But it doesn't have any weight. Because I've been saying no ever since I met her. Ever since I saw her smile and it carried me away in strong rapids leading to a deep, black waterfall.

## 57

The cops hold me in custody until they realize I'm the one who called them. They are swarming the place, yelling orders and talking on walkie-talkies and continuing the evacuation while they wait for crime scene techs to arrive.

A couple ambulances pull up, and medics file into the building. I can't see Frankie or Barton or anybody I know who can give me some kind of information. The cops still remain at my side as if I'm somehow a part of this, but they don't tell me anything.

Then I see a familiar face.

If only it could be Marvel, smiling and relieved and rushing to me with tears of fear and comfort. But it's Mike Harden, the Appleton cop who's kept in touch with all of us at the high school since Artie Duncan's death last summer. He's out of breath and his face looks grim.

"What happened—is Marvel in there—is she okay?"

He shakes his head. "No."

I just wait. I see a look of complete despair on his face.

"Brandon, she died instantly. There was no time—nothing could have saved her."

I can't and don't believe him and I want to say no and my body is trembling, but I'm too weak to scream or even wail.

"How . . . ? Was it Seth? Where is he? What happened?"

Officer Harden doesn't answer my questions. "I'm sorry," he says. "I'm really sorry about Marvel."

Something happens after this—others come around me to help out—some cops or medics or somebody, but I don't know what's happening anymore. Being driven home by a drunk father and then suddenly being smashed by another vehicle feels a lot better than this. Being knocked out at a Halloween party is nothing to this. Diving into the cold water of Lake Michigan out of fear for my life is better than this.

*"For this is the end. I've drowned and dreamt this moment."*

Adele sings in my head and I'm sitting next to Marvel on July Fourth watching the fireworks and vowing to stand tall beside her. But I know the sky has indeed fallen and I was nowhere to be found.

*"There's no hurry, you see. We have all the time in the world."*

# 58

Pieces of information slowly start to come my way, and eventually I can put the whole picture together. Bit by bit, with each new fragment, I wonder how I could have missed it.

"Nobody ever knows when something like this is going to happen. But it's a miracle that more lives weren't lost."

Mike Harden said that to me while I was relaying all the information I had about Seth and what I'd seen at his house. But to me it now seems so obvious. I should have seen this coming.

Frankie managed to find me while I was still at the school. He hugged me and was crying and told me as much as he had seen and heard. Barton joined us, then some teachers.

Soon my mother was there, along with my brothers. I had to talk with more officers. People were surrounding me.

All painting this crimson-stained picture of a hero who stopped everything from happening.

Marvel had texted me, **I'll look for him** just as people were filing into the fine arts theater for the bullying seminar.

Around a thousand students filled the auditorium. That number kept coming up again and again. The entire school. A thousand kids. One thousand lives.

A girl said that Marvel had been with her as they walked into the theater. When she got my text, she told her friend that she needed to do something, then walked back out. A teacher said he saw Marvel walking back out the main entryway to the theater, but he didn't see where she went.

She must have spotted Seth going to the backstage entrance. How did he have access to the backstage? He had been working crew with the drama club. Several kids said that he'd been volunteering since the start of the year. I didn't know that, but how would I? I wasn't part of drama club and I wasn't Seth's best friend.

There was only one reason for Seth Belcher to join stage crew. He'd been planning this for some time. His journal and notes and computer all pointed toward it.

He had hidden a machine gun with belt-fed ammunition in a fake upright piano that was used as a prop in plays. The piano was both light and movable on four wheels, easy to push onstage and pull back off. The top opened up easily, like the top of a storage trunk.

Somehow Seth managed to position the machine gun in the piano so that all he had to do was push it out onto the stage and then unleash the hate that he had been carrying for so long.

They didn't tell me how many rounds there were. But the way people spoke about it . . . Over and over again, the cops acted as if they themselves had just escaped some kind of disaster.

I imagine Marvel following Seth backstage. He had

obviously left the door unlocked. I wonder if at any point she knew what was happening. I wonder if she knew: *This is it. This is my moment.*

I imagine her not thinking at all, however, but just moving and acting.

They said the piano had already been propped open so that you could see the machine gun. Did Marvel say anything to Seth? Did she do anything to him? There wasn't any sign of a struggle.

Did she even have time to think about the truth? That this was what God had spoken to her about?

All those moments.

Maybe a voice whispered in her head and in her heart.

*Marvel, it's time.*

Maybe this great, gentle voice nudged her toward the backstage entrance, where she saw Seth. Maybe the voice kept her calm while she followed him. Kept her strong. Kept her going.

And maybe, probably, she wasn't surprised at the voice, since it had been there the whole time.

Marvel stumbled upon Seth just as he was about to wheel this contraption of death onto the stage. All the students were sitting and he would have had plenty of time for the unthinkable.

Instead, the principal was introducing the speaker when the audience heard a shout. Marvel could not be seen but her voice screamed for everybody to get out, there was a gun and he was going to use it. Then three shots coming from behind the curtain silenced her. Principal Andersen stopped and told everybody to get out of there while he and several other teachers rushed to see what was happening. When they got backstage, they found Marvel dead. Two shots had missed and one had hit her in the head.

The shooter had taken off.

Teachers and students filed out of the building just as they'd practiced. Before the cops could even get there, another shot sounded from a classroom. Seth Belcher killed himself.

Nobody else was involved in the plan. I told the cops where Seth had gotten the gun. I told them he had owed Jeremy Simmons and had even borrowed money from me to pay him. I told them I had no idea what he wanted it for. A few cops kept asking me about this and about my friendship with Seth, as if they thought I might have known. But there were enough people who knew me and knew about my relationship with Marvel to know I had nothing—absolutely *nothing*—to do with this.

*Except I had everything to do with it.*

I kept thinking that. Over and over again. And I kept being reminded of it, too.

*You saved countless lives today, Brandon.*

I know people only wanted to help me, but I couldn't hear anything but pain. I kept thinking of how Marvel walked to her death in the back of the auditorium. Alone and maybe frightened and surely having no idea what was about to happen.

*She wasn't alone.*

I want to believe this. I want to think that Marvella Garcia wasn't alone the moment I first met her and she wasn't alone the moment she took her last breath.

I just wish . . .

I just wish that last breath could have been mine.

# 59

"There you are."

I turn to see Harry walking toward me. I'm standing at the edge of the Fox River near the bridge that connects one side of Appleton to the other. It's a little after six on Saturday evening and the sun is starting to slip down into the west. For a while this afternoon I sat on the sidewalk underneath the bridge, just looking and thinking. And trying unsuccessfully to pray.

"I stopped by your house but your mother said you had left."

I nod. "I needed some air."

"Yeah."

I stare at the massive pillar underneath that's supporting the bridge. It's the place where Artie Duncan's body was found. Lodged against it.

"I'm just trying to understand," I say. "Do you know that Marvel always believed she was going to die? She told me that last summer. She said God spoke to her and *told* her. Do you believe that?"

Harry's eyes focus on me with an alarming intensity. He doesn't seem to grasp what I just said.

"Yes, I know it's crazy," I tell him. "I've spent the last—what?—seven or eight months trying to figure it out. I know it sounds crazy, but I believed Marvel. I just hoped . . . hoped God would change his mind."

"Brandon, she saved the lives of dozens of students. It could have been the worst shooting ever. *Ever.* The two of you—"

"Please—I know. I know. Everybody keeps telling me that. But—does God speak to you? I mean, with a voice you literally hear?"

Harry shakes his head. "No. Sometimes I wish he would. I think we all do. But maybe . . ."

"Maybe what?"

"Maybe this just needed something special. Maybe the evil that was growing had to be stopped."

"I keep telling God to talk. I want to hear him. I want to hear something. Anything. I want to hear him say sorry."

Saying it out loud makes me realize how angry I am. No, not angry. Furious. The same sort of burn that I felt against my father, against Carlos.

*Against those kids who bullied Seth.*

"Everything I've wanted to do with Marvel from the first moment she told me God had spoken to her—every single thing led to this. It led to *me* basically pushing her toward Seth. I helped her die. I'm the only reason she's dead."

"Brandon, look at me, please," Harry says.

His head is tilted slightly, and I study his beard and his eyes behind his glasses. I can tell he's hurting. He looks like someone about to see something bad on television. Wanting to look away but unable to.

"There's a high probability of my saying the wrong thing here, right now," Harry says.

He pauses and lets out a long sigh. I see his chest swell as he breathes in, the tears in his eyes that he's trying to hold back.

"I don't know why bad things happen. But I believe with all my heart that it is the enemy's doing and that we should be angry at him, not at God. I don't believe God wants bad things to happen. I know he doesn't. He grieved when his Son died for us, yet he allowed it."

"Why did he allow this?" I shout. "Why Marvel? Why not me? Why did I have to be the one? The one who led Marvel to Seth?"

"The only thing you did is help Marvel save the lives of all those kids in that auditorium."

The emotion is building again, from my chest and through my throat and once more onto my face. I don't want to cry any more. I'm done crying. I'm done with everything, and I especially want to be done with God. Even if he did save me. Not once but several times.

I try to rip the tears away from my eyes.

Harry puts his hand on my shoulder. "Brandon—come on back home. Okay?"

I shake my head.

"It's not good to be alone, not now. You need to be

surrounded by those you love, okay? There're a lot of people who want to help. They care about you."

"Yeah, I know."

I close my eyes now, wiping my face.

I remember something Marvel said to me. A message she sent to me online.

*"It's important you carry the certainty of being loved with you. Now. And all of your life."*

I don't want to remember this. I want to think I'm alone and unloved and wading through this by myself. The way I was with my father these past few years.

*You still had Devon.*

Marvel and Devon are gone. Everybody I confide in—everybody I end up loving—seems to die.

I want Harry to leave me alone with the river. Leave me to sink into the dark waters. Leave me to this current of rage. Leave me with no answer. At least no answer I want right now.

But I know he's not going to do that.

I nod at him. "I'll go home now," I say.

# 60

This Bible—the words I'm reading on my laptop—have a strange sort of power I don't understand. Before, they've been far more encouraging than words from my mother or the feelings in a Hallmark card. So many that I heard the past year from Marvel or Harry have brought a little bit of peace. But tonight they don't bring comfort at all. They bring judgment and dread. Or maybe that's just how it seems because I feel low and guilty and ashamed.

It feels like I dared God, and he replied. I stood and tried to look him square in the eyes, and he decided to look back. I raised a fist, and he promptly held out his palm. I held my breath, and he softly withdrew his. I said this was worse than death, and he simply proved me wrong.

I failed, so God shook me to get my attention. To give me pause and to shut me up. And that's what I did the moment I took Harry's final suggestion to me before saying good-bye to him—to read through the words God spoke to Job. He told me that was the only known comfort he could think to give to me—to read God's Word. But these words aren't so comforting.

"Who is this that questions my wisdom with such ignorant words? Brace yourself like a man, because I have some questions for you, and you must answer them."

Suddenly I don't want to answer them. I don't want to have this conversation at all.

"Where were you when I laid the foundations of the earth? Tell me, if you know so much."

But I don't know a thing except this anger and this disbelief. Yet the words chip away at them, replacing them with regret.

"Have you ever commanded the morning to appear and caused the dawn to rise in the east? Have you made daylight spread to the ends of the earth, to bring an end to the night's wickedness?"

I haven't done anything except make my demands and whine with my desires and grit my teeth over doubts and anger.

I continue reading, the words shaking me.

"Can you direct the movement of the stars—binding the cluster of the Pleiades or loosening the cords of Orion? Can you direct the constellations through the seasons or guide the Bear with her cubs across the heavens? Do you know the laws of the universe? Can you use them to regulate the earth?"

The glow of the computer screen fills the shadows of the room. I look at the time in the top corner and see that it's past midnight.

I know that my flesh and my blood and my heart and my soul and every breath I take are held in God's hands. He can squeeze me and silence me once and for all. He could hold a finger over my lips and suffocate me. Yet he doesn't, because he loves me and wants me to trust him and obey.

Tomorrow is Easter—no, make that today. It should have been the day Marvel and I would be making our vows and celebrating with a small crowd. Instead there will be a special wake in the evening for her.

I know that anger and confusion and hurt are going to be following me all day and night. But I have to agree with Job. I'm nothing and can't ever find the answers, so I'll just cover my mouth with my hand and hope to do the same with my heart.

"God, help me to breathe better. And to trust you and obey."

# 61

"So let me tell you about Marvel Garcia."

I stand at the pulpit in front of the massive crowd sitting inside the large sanctuary of Appleton Bible Church. There are people standing in the back and along all the sides and even in the balcony. It's Monday morning when I'd usually be at school with the rest of the students at our high school. Many of them surround me right now.

I made it through last night's wake somehow. And right now, I'm doing okay as I try to say a few words about this girl I loved. I want to speak clearly. For everybody in the room. And for Marvel.

If I could say anything I wanted, I'd maybe begin this way.

*There's just something about her smile, something in the way it latches on to you and doesn't let go. It remains in your heart even after she's gone. I can close my eyes and see it. Calling it warm is like saying that about the sun.*

*It's not just bright; it seeks you out. It puts a spotlight on places you didn't even know were there inside of yourself.*

Of course, I don't. I just stand there shaking, trying to control my emotions. I clear my throat and spot Frankie sitting in the front pew along with Barton and so many other classmates. It's comforting to see them there.

I wish I could tell every single one of them all the things swirling around in my head about Marvel.

*There's the way she carries herself, like some kind of angel in search of someone to rescue. Strong and confident, showing no signs of a frightening backstory that might break someone else.*

*There is her fashion sense, not from a book she might have read but instead from one she decided to write for herself. It's not just the seventies thing she always has going on, but the way she wears it. The way she walks. The way she blows in and out like some kind of colorful flag on a battlefield.*

Of course, I don't. I can't. I'm not sure I can say anything. I breathe in, starting to get emotional.

*You can do this—you can get through this.*

"A guy like me might have someone like Marvel walk through the door to their life. But she won't stay long. She won't fall for him. She won't give him her heart. But Marvel sorta did. And the sorta casts a long shadow. The sorta changed me.

"When Marvel walked into my life, I desperately and foolishly tried to hold on to her, in any way I could, even though I knew she wasn't mine to have."

I'm shaking now. I have to wipe yet another one of those tears. I have to.

"Marvel was meant for something else. She belonged to someone else. But that didn't stop me.

"People talk about being reckless in love. I guess that applies here. Marvel was never reckless, however. She simply gave love back.

"But sometimes there's more to the picture. A lot more.

"Sometimes you have to learn the hard way."

I pause for a minute, looking over the students and parents and teachers and so many others in this room. Marvel's aunt Rosa sits with family members on one side of the church. So many people are wiping tears from their eyes. It's nothing short of surreal to be seeing this, especially not long after having done something similar at the smaller funeral for Devon.

"I'm not sure how to follow the other speakers. I shouldn't, really, because what they said is enough. Thank you, pastors, for what you said. Thank you, Principal Andersen. I'm not going to talk at all about what happened. I'm just here to share some thoughts about the girl we're remembering today. I don't want to be up here talking, but I know Marvel would have wanted me to. So I'll try to be half as strong as Marvel was. Hopefully that will be enough."

I look over to see my mother with the rest of my family. I feel bad for Mom, for everything she's been through the last year.

"People have called me a hero, but I'll be honest. I don't know if I could have done what Marvel did. I don't know if I could have been that strong."

I'm not going to share the truth with everybody, the one about Marvel knowing and still remaining strong. I wish everybody in the world knew that strength and that faith.

"I debated about sharing this, but I feel like I should. As

most of you have heard by now, Marvel and I were engaged. This is part of the vows that I was going to make on our wedding day. Here's what I wanted to tell her."

I open the slip of paper that I have on the podium and begin to read.

*"My dearest Marvel:*

*When you first stepped into my life, I was an ordinary guy. I did ordinary things and lived an ordinary life. You were anything but ordinary, however, and the more time I spent with you, the more I realized how special I was, too. Not because I saw myself so differently. No. It's because of how you saw me. And somehow, for some crazy reason, I believed in the things you told me.*

*Sometimes you meet someone and everything clicks. And you realize that you'll do everything in the world to fight to be with that someone."*

I took out some of the things I said just to shorten it up. I don't feel foolish sharing all this in front of these people. I think every single person in this church feels grateful to Marvel. They feel this sad relief that we're only here to commemorate one life and not more.

"'Marvel, I promise you I'll protect you from harm's way,'" I read, my voice breaking a bit in the microphone I'm talking into.

"'Marvel, I will be your knight in shining armor. Maybe a bit dull and maybe not so tall and dark and handsome, but you get the point.'"

Some chuckles in the audience. They're nice to hear.

"'Marvel, I want to spend the rest of my remaining days with you. For better or worse. For whatever comes our way.'"

I look away from the sheet and address the crowd again.

"So obviously I didn't protect her or become her knight or spend my remaining days with her."

This grief—crammed in like a stuffed elevator that's going down. Lots of prayers are coming God's way right now. I hope he hears them all.

"I want to share something else. If you remember anything I shared today, please remember this.

"Marvel kept a blog. I don't know how many read it and how many even knew about it. But I knew about it and read it and loved it. Marvel's aunt gave me her laptop and I discovered this entry on it. It was one that she wrote when I was in trouble—when she thought that she'd be the one standing up here talking about me. These are Marvel's words. They give me a lot of peace and I hope they give you some too."

I read aloud the last blog post Marvel ever wrote.

**"DARKNESS**

You haven't won yet

You haven't found the last word

You haven't suffocated his promises

I cling to them tonight and know they're all I've ever been given

All I have

All that will be

## GLORY

*In the beginning was the Word*

And it's there. Right there. Tonight.

The psalms. The proverbs. The miracles. The majesty.

So I ache because my trust fails. I sink with fear. I burn with restlessness. I question and wonder and worry.

Save me again. Tonight.

And if you can—if there's a way—

Save him. Please, Lord.

Comfort the confused.

Blot out the broken parts.

Fill me once more. Fill me with your promises and your Spirit.

As the song says, help me to find you in the mystery in oceans deep.

Find my faults and let me nail them to your cross.

And free us again.

Let God show mercy by the rising sun coming from heaven.

"To shine on those living in darkness and in the shadow of death."

I love you, Lord. Your arms, your hands, your words, your love.

When the time comes, please be gentle.

Please be quick.

And please, Lord . . . let me be strong.

Let me stand strong knowing where I'm going.

Knowing where I belong. Today and for the rest of the unnumbered days to come.

Let all of us be so strong.

And for all these things spoken and asked and hoped for, I do in the precious, priceless name of your Son, Jesus.

Amen."

I stand there, wiping my eyes and folding the printout I just read, looking out to everybody. I want to add something to these words, say how grateful I was to know Marvel and how grateful I am that she helped point me to God and how he's the only way I'm able to stand right now. But I just nod and smile and then make my way back to my seat.

## 62

The sun hovers over us on the green grass of the cemetery. The same one where Seth was tied to a gravestone and tormented last Halloween. I still can't begin to understand what he did and how I fit inside it. I'm frightened to think about it too much, so I've been trying to block it as much as possible. But being here, surrounded by these headstones and remembering, makes listening to the preacher's words even worse.

There are prayers and words of comfort and Scripture and more encouragement spoken. I receive a hundred hugs. Kisses. Well-wishes. It's like being at some kind of music festival, except I'm the one they've come to see and greet and fall over.

Soon there's only a handful of us left. Marvel's casket is in the ground now. I'm glad it was a closed casket service. I didn't want to see that pretty and vibrant face still and silent. I didn't want my last image to be one that might haunt me for the rest of my life.

My friends slowly drift off. The pastors and Marvel's aunt and cousins and everybody. I'm left with my mother and father and brothers standing there. They're waiting on me. All of them looking so wounded.

I haven't said much to them, especially my father. But as they stand there, I feel this wave of life coming over me. Life that I don't want to waste or ignore and pass by. This breeze of potential.

I walk over and hug my father and I don't let go. I weep against a shoulder I'm not sure I've touched in years. I weep and find some bit of relief in arms that seem unsure at first but then tighten their grip over me.

I don't know if things can get better, but I want to believe they will. God, I need to believe that something good can come from all of this.

# 63

They're all in the next room, unaware I'm standing in the entryway listening to their conversation.

"How in the heck did Seth get that machine gun hidden in a piano?"

Frankie's question is a good one that nobody answers.

Our family room is full of people from my school, some who have never stepped foot in my house before. My brothers and some of their friends are here as well. It was my idea to have people over. It seems like everybody got the memo to come and surround me, but that's okay. Harry was right—it's not good to be alone. I can feel the love, and it's starting to fill this giant hole left behind inside me. I just needed to get some air for a few minutes, so I excused myself.

A girl begins to talk. "I wonder how long he was planning this. Like really. Not just what his journal and everything said, but how long he'd been thinking about it."

This is Gina Broadfoot with the pink hair speaking. She's been around our group ever since going to homecoming with Devon. She was one of the girls who reached out to Marvel and became friends. She was also the girl walking into the fine arts theater with Marvel right before she got my text.

"The guy always was a nut job," Barton says.

This is enough for me to go ahead and enter the room and the conversation.

"Knock it off," I say as I walk toward the group.

I get looks from several others. Everybody is silent, as if they've been caught drinking alcohol behind the school.

Carter says what they're all thinking. "Don't defend him."

"I'm not defending the guy. I just—he died too."

I shake my head and look down. I want to tell them that I hate this kid and I wonder if I'll hate him for the rest of my life. But I feel bad for everything. For not realizing how hurt he obviously was. For not realizing how confused and messed up he was. For not being a better friend. For not figuring out the signs that were so blatant and right in front of me.

*And for being the one to lead Marvel across his psychotic path.*

"His parents are in shock," says a girl named Steph, who came with Gina. "Did you read about them?"

"The parents never know," Barton says. "Oblivious."

As usual, Barton is running his mouth. I wish I could hear Devon's take on this. I wish he were here to share it.

"They said there were five hundred rounds attached to the machine gun," Carter says.

Nobody says anything at the moment. We're probably all picturing the same thing, the scary-looking weapon they've shown on TV. I get chills. Literal chills. A deep sinking feeling in my gut. Then I look over at Alex. We share a knowing glance between us. He was in the auditorium. He and so many others could have died.

I suddenly remember the nightmare I had about Alex. The one where his eyes were shut.

*That's just a coincidence. It's not connected—it can't be.*

But right now I don't know. There are a lot of things I don't quite know.

"They keep showing all these scenes on the news about past shootings," Gina says. "It's horrible."

They're a reminder of this world. The evil out there. But I don't share this. I just want to change the subject.

Mom manages to do that for us when she comes into the room and announces that the pizzas are here.

I think of Devon's funeral and all the food in his parents' house. The endless casserole dishes.

The group of about twenty kids heads into the kitchen. I'm the last to follow them as Frankie waits for me.

"You okay, man?" he asks.

I nod, then ask him something that's been floating around in my head.

"Did I encourage this? With Seth? Getting back? By trying to help him and getting Greg in trouble and all that?"

"Are you serious?" Frankie looks bewildered. "Brandon, seriously—there's nothing you did except try to help. He had issues."

"Maybe it would have gone away," I say. "All of it. Greg and his buddies would have done their thing and then left Seth alone."

"Seth didn't want to be left alone. There were multiple times where he brought things on himself. Who knows—it might have happened sooner without you. You know?"

I sigh and look out a window. It's almost dark outside.

"I so don't want to go back to school tomorrow," I say.

"Yeah, it'll be weird."

We hear screams and laughter in the other room.

"It's going to be weird just being back to normal," I tell him. "And it will, you know. Things will go back to normal. They always do."

"They're supposed to. They *have* to."

I nod at Frankie. I'm about to head into the kitchen when I notice a framed picture somebody put on the end table next to the couch. A blue lamp used to stand there before I used it over my father's head. Now another lamp is in its place. A far less bulky one.

I pick up the picture and look at Marvel. She's smiling, wearing her knit wool hat with her long hair pouring out of it. Someone must have taken this picture at school.

"Gina brought that," Frankie says. "Pretty good one, huh?"

Not a care in the world. That's what her smile says, even though I knew the truth. Such peace inside it, even though I knew a war raged around her.

I want to stand there and study it and be left alone, but Frankie takes the frame and puts it back on the table.

"Come on," he tells me, pulling me toward the kitchen. "You gotta eat. Okay. We're in training."

"Training? For what?" I ask.

"To battle our sorrows. We got enough of them and they're not going to go away, right? So we need fuel to figure things out. And pizza sounds good to me."

I nod and follow him.

Frankie's a smart kid. He's one of the good ones, and I'm glad he's still in my life.

# 64

Everything about this morning is different. From the moment I wake up so early the sun hasn't even started to think of rising, to eventually finding my entire family, including my father, waiting for me in the kitchen for a full breakfast. Frankie joins us. I'm not particularly hungry, but I try to eat. I try to remain in training, as Frankie said.

It's been a week since everything happened, and the first day everybody will be back at school. Since my Honda Pilot still remains MIA, Frankie drives us to the spot where we'll park. We plan to walk the rest of the way. And we won't be alone.

When we make the first turn onto the main street in Appleton that we take to school, I see the group we'll be joining. The sidewalks are full of people. Students. Not the usual handful I see walking to school every day, but dozens. Maybe even hundreds, lining both sides of the street heading all the way toward downtown Appleton.

Frankie slows his Toyota and parks it in someone's driveway. On a morning like this, nobody is going to mind.

This morning, the country is watching our little town. So

we've decided we're going to show them and the rest of the world. We're going to show them exactly what Marvel wrote. The darkness hasn't won. It's never going to win.

As I get out of the car, a wave of joyful grief rushes over me and fills my eyes and my soul. I look back to Frankie, who is still smiling but appears as though he might cry too. A quick sweep of the crowd reveals a lot of people I know. People like Barton, of course. Gina with a group of her eccentric friends. Taryn is there with her group. I see Harry and Sarah with their boys. Good old Phil is there with them. The Teeds. Mr. and Mrs. Menke, Barton's parents. Mr. Midkiff and Mrs. Schwartzburg and so many others. The cop—Mike Harden—is there in plain clothes. Nick the detective is next to him, and he actually looks cleaned up and not so disheveled today.

Then I see my brothers walking toward me, with my parents following. They all look pretty emotional, especially Carter. He's bawling. The big baby. I hug him first.

My mother clings to me; then I hug my father. Again.

All of us are here to remember Marvel. And to thank God for her one single brave act.

The massive group starts to walk. Not on the sidewalks, but down the center of the street. It's surreal to be in the middle of it, this rushing river breaking through the dams of fear and darkness.

With each step, I realize I'm changing. I realize that something is here, something bigger than me, something truly all-powerful and all-knowing and all-loving. He is the only kind of ALL I need. And I desperately ask God to help me walk this distance with his strength. He knows I need it.

When I look around again to see all the students, I realize

that many of them are wearing some type of seventies fashion like a wide hat or a wild-looking shirt or a flowing skirt, all in Marvel's memory. It makes me laugh.

A lot of them wouldn't be here today without Marvel.

*And you, Brandon. And you too.*

A part of me realizes that I will always—*always*—be the guy wanting to help and rescue and defend. Whatever that means. In whatever fashion I can.

I glance over my shoulder at Mike Harden, who helped track down Uncle Carlos. Then at Nick Hamilton, who rescued me from the waters of Lake Michigan. They're heroes. Like so many others.

We walk and I see Marvel's smile. And suddenly I can hear her voice in another one of those blogs. I'm not sure if it's because I just read it last night or if it's because God is giving me this or maybe because I'm just making this up on my own. Figuring out how to battle these sorrows.

Actually, I am sure. God's giving me these words as I walk at the head of the line back to Appleton High. Back to a place where evil lashed out.

I can hear her voice speaking the words she wrote not long ago.

> Joy ankle-deep
>
> We wade through holding hands

I see the students surrounding me holding hands, my brothers, my parents. I forget the man rule and grab Frankie's and hold it tight.

> The sun doesn't set or rise but hovers like a humming-bird
>
> I close my eyes and know
>
> The darkness won't be there
>
> One day it won't be there
>
> But you will be

The bright lamp in the sky has a giant spotlight on us—the day just can't be any more beautiful. Cars and trucks and SUVs are parked along the road and they honk while others hold school banners and pictures of Marvel. Some take pictures and video. I know that Marvel is right. Darkness hasn't won. And we're sending that message to the rest of the world in the same way so many others have done the same. Unifying and coming together and showing everybody.

> And on this lovely day
>
> We will replay these sights and sounds
>
> Perfect and unfolding and grateful for salvation
>
> Grateful for life

We near the buildings for the first time. I haven't been here since everything happened. A slight fear claws at my throat, but I look back and see the endless lines of students and teachers and families. To say I feel supported is an understatement. But they're not here for me. *We* are here for everybody.

I hear Marvel's voice continue to speak in my mind.

Eternity

Endless, everlasting, everything we could dream for and a million times more

Singing and loving and laughing and worshiping together

Celebrating our rescue

This lovely day replayed day after day

A lovely day that never ends

---

I step into the school parking lot and see more vehicles lining each side. More official ones now. Fire trucks and squad cars and ambulances. There are more spectators, too—parents and family members and media and so many I can't see them all. More applause. More reminders of Marvel.

We are not alone in this. I know that. All we can do is keep walking and keep smiling and keep believing that the dark will not extinguish the light.

*God, please have mercy on all of us.*

I think that maybe, hopefully, Marvel can see this. If she does, surely she is smiling.

She never stopped believing. And her only hesitation came when I tried to steal her away.

The school doors are open.

*We will never forget, Marvel. Never.*

# 65

"Hurts, doesn't it?"

I turn to the voice and see a bearded figure in the shadows of the unlit store. Phil. It's like he came out of nowhere.

"How long have you been here?" I ask.

"Long enough. You doin' okay?"

I mutter a yes, but I guess he knows I'm lying. It's the first Saturday after being back at school. Life does go on as "normal" to some degree.

I wonder if he's going to try to provide some kind of counsel or encouragement.

"I want to tell you something," he says as he walks up close to me. "Okay? I'll just say it once, and you can do with it what you want. Got it?"

I nod. His words are stern enough to know not to test him, yet his tone is still easygoing, like some kind of cool Santa. The early morning sun is soaking in through the windows and shining on the wall behind him, hitting the big poster of Jimi Hendrix that hovers there as if the guitarist is playing backup while Phil is the lead singer.

"You see things, right?" Phil asks.

I don't say anything, because I'm not sure at first what he means.

"I know—you probably don't want to say anything," he continues. "You'll sound crazy. But hey—look who you're talking to. I'm Phil. The guy everybody thinks fried his brain on drugs and is just livin' life smiling and looking at the stars and saying, 'Cool, man.' But they're wrong. I mean—yes, I did my share of drugs, but I still have every brain cell up here. It's just that I see things. And I know you do too."

"How do you know?" I ask.

Phil smiles. "What if you'd been doing something your whole life? Like one of those music producers who's been working since the seventies? They've seen and heard it all. So they know—they just *know* when someone special comes along. It's not just what they hear and see, but their soul tells them. And in my case—in our case—this is a lot more . . . well, specific."

I'm still not sure what he's saying. "You see things? Like what kinds of things?"

"I see the future. I see things that might happen. But the most important word to remember is *might*. Got it?"

No, I don't. Even after everything that's happened, this still sounds too crazy. Now Phil is seeing things too? What's next? Harry will tell me he's going to be blasting off into space for the nearest wormhole?

"Remember the time I showed up out of the blue while you were walking home late at night? It's 'cause I'd seen something. One of my 'trailers.' I call 'em that because—well, I hate the word *vision*. It sounds so biblical. But I know that this seeing is something God gave me and I've used it for good. Well, once I finally let go and accepted it and didn't think I was losing my mind."

I remember the night he's talking about. I just assumed it was because of Artie Duncan's death and Phil simply being kind, seeing a kid he knew and offering him a lift.

"I saw something that—well, it wasn't pretty," Phil says. "I didn't see the *who* but I sure saw the *what*. So I showed up. And then there was the time when I made sure you didn't do something stupid with Señor Carlos. Remember? When I showed up in Marvel's parking lot? Again, out of the blue."

I've always wondered how he knew I was there that day and why he'd been spying on me.

"In your dream, you saw me there? In that parking lot?"

Phil heads over to the desk as if he just thought of something, then digs through the records with his back to me. He finds what he's looking for, then turns to me.

"I saw the windows of your car bashed in and your throat cut," he says without much expression.

"Yikes," I say.

He nods. "Yeah. So I'm crazy, huh? Except, Uncle Carlos did take you. Twice, in fact. See—it's not like I know when the trailers are gonna come. And I can't always change things. Right?"

*Am I dreaming now? Having a vision? Or watching a supernatural trailer?*

Phil keeps talking.

"Your mind is racing. I get it. I didn't have anybody to

explain it to me. But God chased after me a long time before I finally bent my knees and asked for help. You've already been there. And you can do something with this gift."

"It's a gift?" I say.

"Yes, Brandon. Of course it's a gift. Being able to help someone or some awful situation before it happens? What do you think?"

He puts on some music, and drums suddenly fill the silence. Phil smiles and nods his head up and down. Then the warm guitars and keyboards burst through. It's an oldie, of course. Something from the seventies, surely.

I'm about to speak but he holds up his hand and points at the speakers as if to get me to listen carefully.

*"Because there's no explaining what your imagination can make you see and feel."*

The song has a groovy, laid-back sort of feel, much like Phil himself. I see that grin of his behind the beard and those wide eyes, as if he's got so many stories to tell.

"'Hypnotized' by Fleetwood Mac," he says. "An oldie, before their classic lineup. But this one's always been a favorite of mine. The older I get, the more I think of it as my theme song. You know? 'Seems like a dream.' Yeah. You know."

If he still smoked pot, I have a feeling Phil would light up right now and offer me a hit. A part of me *wants* a hit. I want to make sense of everything.

When the song ends, he switches albums, and even I recognize this one. Still Fleetwood Mac. He puts on "Dreams," and I hear Stevie Nicks and think about Marvel.

"So tell me," Phil says, turning the volume down so we

can talk. "Did you ever have trailers about Marvel? About what happened at school?"

"Yeah. I didn't know what they meant or anything. But I saw it."

"What did you see?"

I try to remember the different dreams. They all blur together.

"I just remember that in some of them, Marvel was with me. But she was sad. Lots of people were sad. There was this really awful feeling. A sick feeling like something horrible had happened."

Phil nods and gets contemplative again. "You saw the *could've been*. You know?"

I breathe in and then let out a sigh.

"You thought you were seeing something good, right? And maybe you thought that was the right thing—to have this amazing girl still at your side. But life didn't work out that way. That girl—the same one who used to dance in our store to Stevie Nicks, the one who should've been born in the seventies, one I would've wanted to drive around on my motorcycle—she saved the lives of countless kids. Maybe a hundred or more."

I feel the tears coming, burning once more. "I couldn't do anything. I didn't know what I was seeing. What the dreams meant."

He walks over to me and puts his hands on my shoulders. "It's okay," he says.

In the background the male voice is now singing about being down and never going back. I can relate.

"Ever heard of Flannery O'Connor, the writer?" Phil asks.

I shake my head, suddenly wishing I'd paid more attention at school.

"She once said this. 'Don't let me ever think, dear God, that I was anything but the instrument for your story—just like the typewriter was mine.'"

For a moment he lets the quote sink in. It reminds me of something Marvel might have said.

Then, "Listen to me," Phil says, looking squarely at me. "You got a gift. Use it, Brandon. Use it for God. For his glory. You got that? There's a war out there, and it's only gonna get worse."

He moves back to the counter. "Remember, buddy. Yesterday's gone. But tomorrow's gonna be here soon."

He turns up the stereo as "Don't Stop" begins, and then walks out. I let out a laugh, hearing the song, thinking he's been planning this for a while. But even if he has, and even if it's a little obvious, I can't help but feel goose bumps.

I lean against a row of records and then look around. Fleetwood Mac jams and I can feel the bass booming in my gut.

I look at that door again and remember Marvel walking through it.

"'All I want is to see you smile,'" the singer says.

Yeah.

One day maybe. One day.

I hope it'll be better than before. But Phil and all the Fleetwood Macs are right. Yesterday is gone. But tomorrow's gonna be here and yeah. I can't stop.

*I won't, Marvel. I promise.*

# 66

The first official week of summer I decide to ride my bike to the record store. I need to get into shape and the weather is perfect, so I don't have any excuse. I have a brand-new Ford Escape sitting in my driveway that I have driven exactly four times. I still don't really know what to do with it. It's like I won some grim sort of lottery after Marvel died. People have given me and my family so much. The Escape came around graduation. It came simply "from the town of Appleton." I tried to give it to Marvel's aunt, but it turned out she received a car too.

I ride my bike past the bike park where I first saw Seth getting beat up. Once again I wonder if I could have done more. But maybe if I had, I would have been late for work or not gone in at all. Maybe I wouldn't have met Marvel that day and gotten her to come back and work at the store.

Maybe nobody would have died. Maybe a hundred students would have died.

Maybes. Possibilities. I don't know.

God had a plan. A purpose.

I sit there on my bike, feeling very alone, wondering what the future holds.

I know something. My faith will not waver. It won't waver because Marvel's never wavered.

Whatever the future holds in college and the rest of my life, I will be strong. I will be faithful.

*I will go where you want me to go, God. Show me the way. Show me wherever I need to go.*

I won't stay in my seat. I won't stand still. I won't hold back. I won't let go.

Because Marvel didn't.

*God, speak to me. The same way you spoke to her.*

I'm ready to know what I'm meant to do. Whatever it might be.

# 67

The first weekend of August, I spend three days in Chicago with Frankie and Barton while Lollapalooza takes over a good portion of the city. We stay at a nearby hotel, nothing really fancy but still expensive.

I have fun but it's not the same as last year. Not in the slightest. Last year the surprise was finding Marvel at my side. To hear the music and know that she was near. Now the songs seem to bounce off me. There's an empty space next to me in the throngs of people.

Sunday starts with rain, and Barton and Frankie decide to stay back at the hotel. They were out late while I went to bed fairly early. The party scene is just not my thing. I can endure it, but I also need to escape sometimes. They tell me they'll find me later that afternoon.

I don't tell Barton and Frankie I want to see London Grammar. The band is too slow for them. But that's okay.

I arrive early and wait near the front of the stage. The rain stays away for a while, with the sun even peeking out of the clouds a handful of times.

When the three-person band finally comes out and starts to play, I feel an awesome wave of sadness covering me. I think of holding Marvel on that perfect summer day. Of looking up at the sky and knowing she was near and feeling like anything was possible. *Anything*.

I know something now. Grief is a cloud that can come at any moment on any day.

Everything about the band reminds me of Marvel. It's just not right that I'm here on my own. It's not fair that she's not right here next to me.

I think of that miraculous moment when, in the middle of the concert, everybody simply disappeared except Marvel and me. The band continued to play and sing about heaven, but we were the only two in the massive field. It was nighttime, but everything suddenly lit up. Then the song ended and the darkness came back.

*Maybe that can happen again and I can find my soul mate waiting for me.*

Instead, it starts to rain. Then pour. All of us in the crowd are immune to the weather. A lot of people have rain gear, but I'm standing here getting soaked. It feels good to listen to the female singer's glorious voice as the heavens open up and pour down on us.

*I miss you, Marvel.*

With every beat and every word and every song.

A slow song by the band begins during the rain, and then . . .

Something happens.

Right when the singer says, "Keep it together," I blink and then feel the drizzle stop. Another blink and the sky above is sparkling, vibrant blue. London Grammar keeps playing and the music keeps going, but I'm alone.

*Keep it together, Brandon.*

It's a perfect day and I see a pulsing sort of light shining from behind me. So I turn and see the field, the biggest section of Grant Park. It's empty. Not one soul is—

*No. There's someone.*

In the center, directly behind me but maybe fifty yards back, stands some guy in a white concert T-shirt and baggy shorts. He's wearing sunglasses and a sombrero. The hat is probably annoying for those standing behind him, but it's perfect for this rainy day.

*But it's not raining anymore.*

The song is building, with guitar and drums flowing, and all I can do is stare at this lone figure in the field. It looks like there's an image of some guy smiling on his shirt, but from here I can't see who. I actually wave like some idiot, but there's no reaction. Then I see the guy's hand go up, like anybody's might at a concert, but seeing him do this all on his own seems strange.

"What are you afraid of?" a voice sings.

Then the song ends, and just like last summer the crowd returns with the dark sky and the drizzle. I turn around but can't see any sign of the guy.

Nothing weird happens for a few hours. Nothing except rain. Lots and lots of rain. I meet up with Frankie and Barton, who are with a bigger group, and they all want to stay to see

Young the Giant and then Kings of Leon. I'm already soaked, so a little more rain isn't going to hurt.

Suddenly I see that sombrero again. Maybe there are others wearing them, but I know it's the same guy because I see his T-shirt. He turns just then and catches me staring at his shirt. He steps closer.

"You like the Smiths?" he asks.

I shake my head. "Never heard of them."

"What? Seriously?"

I think Harry might have told me about them at one time. "They from the eighties?"

"Buckley here is a retro guy," another one of the guys in the group says about sombrero guy. "And a music snob."

"I'm not a snob," he says. "I just have really good taste."

He nods and seems nice enough, even though the hat is really ridiculous.

"You'd probably like my boss," I tell him.

"Yeah? Why's that?"

"He runs a record store. He loves eighties tunes."

"Cool," the guy says. "My uncle got me into music. I collect vinyl."

"Then you'd love our store. Fascination Street Records."

He laughs. "I guess your boss does love the eighties. That's The Cure."

"I saw them here last summer," I say.

"Yeah? Me too. They were awesome."

We talk about Lolla, and he walks with the rest of our group down to the field to get a decent location for Young the Giant. I stay near the guy, who tells me his name is Chris, trying to see if any more weird things happen. Like frogs falling from the sky or UFOs suddenly landing or maybe some kind of weird portal opening up.

But nope. Nothing strange happens.

We wait for the band, a mob of wet, muddy souls. Endless. The weather gets worse and the light starts to fade away.

Sometime before the end of the night sombrero guy has disappeared into the crowd. I make sure to remember his name.

*Chris Buckley.*

Something tells me it won't be the last time I run into him.

# 68

My body aches as I sit at the top of a brand-new brick driveway that swings down the hill and curves toward the road. It's been a four-week job with a local landscape company. I swear we've put in ten thousand bricks. In the past month I've probably lost ten pounds and then added another twenty in muscle. I'm ripped and ready to start college in another week and feeling like a healthy soul.

I'm just sitting and drinking a Gatorade and talking to God. I realize now that you don't always have to "pray"; you can just have a conversation. And even though there aren't words that you literally hear coming back at you, I don't believe it's a one-sided conversation. Not in the least.

I wipe the sweat off my forehead and glance up to the sky. I think about Marvel again. Like always.

One day, I would like to ask God why he put Marvel in my life. Was it to allow me to love and support her during the last year of her life on this earth? Was it to be a friend walking alongside her and pointing a flashlight in front of her feet?

Was it to help her live out the true destiny she had been called to by God?

I don't know.

Some days, when it's silent and I'm wondering about what life is going to be like tomorrow or the next day, I think about Marvel. How she loved me. How she was my friend. How she helped me live in dark times. How she allowed me to see so much more. Not only in the world but also in myself.

Maybe God put her in my life to remind me I'm lovable.

For most of my life, I never really thought too much about that. Being loved. I just accepted that maybe I couldn't be and maybe that was okay and maybe that's just the way life happens to be. Some fathers are monsters and so are some people out there and bad things happen.

But good things happen too. Good things like Marvel. Her heart. Her smile. Her faith.

Every part of me intends to carry the love that Marvel showed and remind myself it's the same sort of unconditional love God has for me. Except his is perfect and comes every moment of every day.

Man, that's hard to fully believe. But I will try. I will try.

There's so much else to think about. This giant *next step* that's coming with moving on campus to go to UIC and all that. But still I'm right here with Marvel.

*"Stay awake while the dark despair sings its lullabies to the world*

*"Stay awake to stay strong"*

The words of her blog posts remain with me. I have all of them memorized by now. They still speak to me even in this silence.

Sometimes I don't like thinking about her. I don't like knowing. Remembering this girl I met with bright eyes and smooth skin and lips I kissed.

Memories are like light. They can slip through cracks you can't seal. They can be bright enough to see in the distant sky. Yet unlike the sun, they don't slip away. They remain, even when the darkness comes.

I guess we have to choose what to do with them. Will they keep the light shining in the darkness? Or will they simply provide shadows to follow behind us?

I still hear her songs and feel her joy and remember her coming beside me. For this short little breath of time.

I'm better for it. I know this. But that doesn't mean I don't miss her.

I'll miss her for the rest of my life. Knowing she's in a better place, a place I'm heading to, a place where I'll find her again.

A place she knew she would be seeing soon.

I bet it's even more glorious than she thought it'd be.

I'll see you inside those golden gates, Marvel. And I'll tell you everything I've seen along the way.

*"The Lord has done this,
and it is* **MARVELOUS** *in our eyes."*
PSALM 118:23 (NIV)

✟

*"O Lord my God, you have performed many* **WONDERS** *for us. Your plans for us are too numerous to list. You have no equal. If I tried to recite all your wonderful deeds, I would never come to the end of them."*
PSALM 40:5

✟

*"Everyone was gripped with great wonder and* **AWE**, *and they praised God, exclaiming, 'We have seen amazing things today!'"*
LUKE 5:26

✟

*"Yet what we suffer now is nothing compared to the* **GLORY** *he will reveal to us later. For all creation is waiting eagerly for that future day when God will reveal who his children really are."*
ROMANS 8:18-19

# ACKNOWLEDGMENTS

Thanks...

To Sharon, Kylie, Mackenzie, and Brianna for surrounding me with beauty and love.

To my parents and in-laws for never telling me to get another job (at least to my face!).

To my extended family, who always make me feel like I'm doing something special.

To Meg Wallin, for believing in Brandon and Marvel. I hope you like how it turned out!

To LB Norton, for continuing to wade down these strange and wonderful writing waters with me. And for putting up with my tendency toward alliteration.

To Erin Smith, for cleaning up the little messes made, and for pointing out how many times Brandon nods and smiles.

To David Carlson, for such a fabulous set of covers. And to Dean Renninger, for making the interior pages so welcoming to read.

To Claudia Cross, in times of feast and famine!

To NavPress & Tyndale & Lucas Lane. I couldn't find a fourth publisher, however . . .

To Don Pape, for always calling and wishing me a happy birthday despite what my sales figures might be.

To the town of Batavia, where my wife and I worked and where our girls went to school. Thank you for being the inspiration for the setting of The Books of Marvella. I changed the name simply because you're too wonderful to ever turn evil like Appleton does. (Future series spoiler alert!!)

To all my readers, especially those who have embraced this series. Thank you for your patience in finally seeing how things turn out.

And to Chris Buckley. Welcome back.

# AUTHOR NOTE
## (WITH SPOILERS, SO BE WARNED)

So I need to share some things with you. Not just to convince you I'm not a cruel and vicious person, but also because I really want to share my creative process and the heart behind this series.

A couple of things happened the day I wrote the scene where Brandon discovers the planned horror that is happening at Appleton High School and then races back. I was looking up something about the Columbine High tragedy when I discovered a lengthy documentary of the way the shooting unfolded. I watched and was overcome with sadness. Tears flowed. Then, right after writing my scene, I went to work out, just to do a little cardio since I sit all day. I was thinking of my story and the school shooting and then of Marvel and of Brandon and I started getting teary-eyed again. Just thinking about them, about made-up characters.

These people mean more to me than you could ever know.

From the very beginning I wanted to write about a young woman who had heard God's voice and who became a hero doing his will. I know there will surely be people who say,

"How could you actually kill her?" but Marvel told us this would happen from the start. Her death shouldn't have been a surprise. God preventing it would have been. But the thing that even I didn't see coming was how Brandon was the key to Marvel becoming the hero. In a sense, he pulled the trigger. And by helping to do so, he allowed Marvel to prevent dozens of lives from being taken.

Even though school shootings have unfortunately become common in the news these days, they still always seem to come out of the blue. But then again, they don't. Sometimes there seems to be no reasonable answers—maybe the kids were bullied and maybe they simply have psychological issues and maybe there's no explanation.

I don't want to be glib and simply say it's evil. But The Solitary Tales and The Books of Marvella both deal with evil in this world and with spiritual warfare. And I truly believe that Satan takes delight in the catastrophes in our lives.

✛ ✛ ✛

I believe you can't *will* a good story to life. You can force yourself to sit down and write. You can write detailed outlines and character notes. But none of those things will create a soulful and heartfelt story.

Yet one Saturday in January of 2013, I spent several hours trying to unearth some kind of gem. I wanted to find something special. And I even prayed to God to give me some sort of idea.

I don't usually pray this sort of prayer, for a couple of reasons. Yes, I pray all the time for my writing, but I don't ordinarily make a request like this. One reason is because I get numerous story ideas *daily*. The hard part isn't coming up with an idea. The difficulty comes in picking which one to write.

The other reason I don't ask God to give me some special idea is because it's a Christian publishing cliché. When I worked at a publishing house, I heard so many people say, "God gave me this story." Then they followed that up with "So will you publish it?" Or, since I've been writing full-time, they'll say, "So I think you need to help me write it."

Yet on this Saturday, I found myself searching and praying. But there was a specific reason behind my—well, let's call it anxious passion.

The night before I'd had what the intro to the *Wide World of Sports* used to call the thrill of victory and the agony of defeat. This had come in a manner of minutes, too. I'd been waiting to hear about a collaboration project that I'd been working on for a while with a big-name author. A friend of mine too. The proposals had gone out the month before and we were waiting, getting rejections back. It was one of those periods in my full-time writing life when I needed some kind of door to open. A *God-please-give-us-something* sort of period. So a door finally opened. A great publisher loved the idea and wanted to move ahead with a three-book deal.

Their offer was fair and received with celebration by me. My bestselling writer friend had agreed to split the agreement 50–50, so I knew what amount I'd be paid to write the series of novels. I called the author up and gave the update on the acceptance and the offer. The voice on the other end simply laughed and scoffed. Instead of agreeing to the 50–50 split, he suggested that I do the deal (a series of novels that I would completely write, with input) for an 86–14 split. I guess I don't need to tell you who would get the 14 percent.

My wife and my parents were more incensed than I was. They were angry *for* me. I politely turned it down and then closed the door on this project. I was simply frustrated once again at the reality of publishing.

So the next day I wanted to think of something, anything. Maybe it was to try to rinse my mouth of the foul taste from this previous project idea.

That morning, I thought of Marvel's story. It all just seemed to come to me. In one burst. I wrote down as much as I could about the idea. I waited to see if I'd like it as much the following day and the one after that. It just so happened that I continued to love the idea more and more.

✤ ✤ ✤

One name came to mind with this series about Marvel. Meg Wallin.

Meg was the editor at NavPress who acquired The Books of Marvella series. On April 24 of 2012 (the year before the above incident happened), she sent me an e-mail through my website introducing herself. In it she said the following:

> I recently stumbled across *Solitary* in the bookstore and couldn't put it down. I just finished *Gravestone* and *Temptation* this past weekend, and I have to say, I'm really disappointed that I have to wait until January for *Hurt*!

Well, it's not every day that I receive such kind words from an editor in the industry whom I don't know (this might have been the first time). She simply wanted to talk, and that conversation led to our working together.

At first I tried to do a Christian Hunger Games series (don't roll your eyes—okay, fine, roll them). It actually was a really fun storyline. If you want to really roll your eyes, the idea came from Coldplay's *Mylo Xyloto* album. It was a cross between *The Hunger Games* and *The Bachelor*. No joke. (Maybe the reason it never went anywhere.)

So I pitched this new idea to Meg, and she loved it. I wrote out a detailed synopsis and she came back with questions and thoughts that helped to shape it. It went through the proposal process and was accepted.

Marvel and Brandon would soon see the light of day.

✦ ✦ ✦

Flash forward to fall of 2014. After finishing the third book in this series, I handed it in and asked about payment. I got an ominous e-mail back from the publisher.

"Can we talk on the phone? I'm looking at sales for *Marvelous* and have concerns."

*Uh-oh.*

I've been in publishing long enough to know if they want to talk to me on the phone it's usually not a good thing. *Especially* if they want to talk about sales.

They didn't have a choice—the sales were low and they couldn't justify continuing the series with books three and four (book two was already too far down the pike to stop). So I got the rights.

Never did I think, *Well, that's the end of the series.* I planned to write book four and then publish the last two. So hopefully you're reading this right now with a beautiful-looking copy of *Glory* in your hands.

✛ ✛ ✛

Obviously I needed to finish Marvel's story. Every single plot point heads to the final act in *Glory*. Now you see the whole picture. Or at least most of the picture in Marvel's story.

So what's next? Well, Chris and Brandon have met. If you don't know Chris Buckley, check out my other YA series, The Solitary Tales. (If you missed that Chris was the one Brandon met at Lollapalooza—well, I thought that was glaringly obvious and I even got someone to call out his last name.)

I can see their paths crossing in the future. In fact, I have that already plotted out, too. You know me, right?

I do know there are mysteries that were left dangling. Otis, for instance. What *was* happening in the warehouse or behind his house in the woods? Is there more to Appleton than meets the eye? And what about Lee Fleisher?

I know the answers. That's all I'll say. My hope is that I'll be able to tell more of the story. With Chris and Brandon. They have a few things in common, don't they? Maybe they can help each other in ways they don't even know. Maybe they can—

Well, I'll keep the maybes to myself. At least most of them.

✦ ✦ ✦

So back to Marvel and her journey. It leads to the age-old question so many ask:

Why does God allow tragedies to happen?

A lot of great pastors and Christian speakers address this. I found two very encouraging speeches that happened after school shootings.

Author Lee Strobel gave a message on this topic right after the awful shooting at a movie theater in Aurora, Colorado. Here's something he said:

> "[God] offers us the two very things we need when we're hurting: peace to deal with our present and courage to deal with our future. How? *Because he has conquered the world!* Through his own suffering and death, he has deprived this world of its ultimate power over you. Suffering doesn't have the last word anymore. Death doesn't have the last word anymore. God has the last word!"

In the memorial service message Franklin Graham gave in Littleton, Colorado, for Columbine High School victims on April 25, 1999, he said this:

> "I pray that every one of you will experience God's comfort as you turn to him, for God loves you and he shares in this suffering. You see, God understands loss—the loss of this world to sin. The loss of his Son,

the Lord Jesus Christ, as he hung on Calvary's cross, as he gave his life for our sins."

Both of their speeches really put things in perspective. For those grieving, I know it might not be so easy to simply receive God's comfort. I cannot imagine the suffering families have gone through. I hope that in no way have I dishonored God or the families of victims through telling this story.

The goal with these books wasn't to glorify the darkness but to celebrate the light that triumphs over it. I believe Marvel's testimony does this. I love how she shines throughout all four books.

I want to end by once again thanking everybody who has taken this journey with me. These are novels and they're obviously fiction. Real life is a lot more painful and murky and dark. But that doesn't mean the themes and emotions and faith in these stories aren't real. They are. Very much so.

# PLAYLISTS

## A BIRTHDAY CELEBRATION THROUGH THE DECADES
40s "Le Vie en Rose" by Edith Piaf
50s "Love Me Tender" by Elvis Presley
60s "God Only Knows" by the Beach Boys
70s "Leather and Lace" by Stevie Nicks
80s "Lovesong" by The Cure
90s "Wonderwall" by Oasis
00s "Chasing Cars" by Snow Patrol
10s "XO" by Beyonce

## A GLORIOUS PLAYLIST
1. "Planets of the Universe (demo)" by Fleetwood Mac
2. "White Foxes (Man Without Country remix)" by Susanne Sundfør
3. "All Our Endless Love" by The Bird and the Bee (featuring Matt Berninger)
4. "Interlude (live)" by London Grammar
5. "I See Fire (Kygo remix)" by Ed Sheeran
6. "Beating Heart" by Ellie Goulding
7. "While I'm Still Here" by Nine Inch Nails
8. "The Whisperer" by David Guetta (featuring Sia)
9. "Sedated" by Hozier
10. "Lovely Day (bonus track)" by Alt-J
11. "Don't Stop" by Fleetwood Mac
12. "Nuvole Bianche" by Ludovico Einaudi
13. "Disfruto" by Carla Morrison
14. "Stay Awake" by London Grammar
15. "Going Home" by Asgeir
16. "Oblivion" by M83 (featuring Susanne Sundfør)

# "SPIRIT LEAD ME

**WHERE MY TRUST IS WITHOUT BORDERS
LET ME WALK UPON THE WATERS
WHEREVER YOU WOULD CALL ME"**

"OCEANS" BY HILLSONG UNITED